History of Us

History of Us

A Friendships and Festivals Romance

Stacey Agdern

TULE
PUBLISHING

Dedication

This book is dedicated to Jane Agdern, Linda Gerstman, and Beverly Jenkins.

Each of you helped me frame my view of history – as a child, as a student, and as an author. It is because of each of you that I've written this book.

Chapter One

ONE MORE CARD, and she'd be finished.

Anna Cohen finished writing the reference on the index card, put her pen down and took a deep breath. She'd been working late into the night, and had finally finished the first part of the exhibition.

It was such a relief. She stretched behind her desk, put her annoyingly straight brown hair into a bun, and sat back. The pressure was off, at least for now. Working on one of Jemima Kellerman's exhibits at the Manhattan Museum of Jewish History was a great boost for her career for sure.

As she was about to check her email, she heard a knock on the door of her tiny office. "Come in," she said.

"Are you finished with the cards?"

Her boss. Head curator. Jemima Kellerman.

This was big.

Anna straightened her skirt and stood, carefully moving the second of her cups of tea out of the way so that she wouldn't knock them all over the reference books she'd been using. Details were important. "Yes," she said as she headed toward the door, grabbing the cards from her desk.

Her boss stood on the threshold, just beyond the open door, glossy dark hair hanging just below her shoulders, brown eyes focusing on Anna, her skin as pale as the tips of her French manicure. "Anna, you look like you've pulled an all-nighter."

Jemima was a *personality* to be sure. However, the head curator had her working on interesting projects that were in line with Anna's areas of interest, just seen through a different lens. But no matter what she felt about the projects her boss assigned her, it was important that Anna do her job right, respect the history and the people who'd lived it.

"I have," she said. "I got so lost in the stories, I needed to make sure I got the details right." She passed over the cards and waited.

One. Two.

Anna couldn't watch as Jemima flipped through them. If she did, she'd ask too many questions and interrupt her boss.

Finally.

Jemima looked up, her eyes bright. "These are perfect. I'm so glad you're on my team here. After lunch you'll come to my office and we'll talk about the next stage, hmm?"

The excitement and exuberance in Jemima's voice was what Anna had dreamed of hearing from her boss. The praise in those first two sentences gave Anna wings—and courage.

Strike while the iron was hot?

"Yes, absolutely," Anna replied. "That sounds great, although…"

"Yes?"

Anna held her breath, nervous but ready. It was time. "If I have any ideas of my own for exhibits, would you be interested in listening to them?"

Jemima nodded. "Absolutely. Work up a proposal and bring it to me when you're ready."

"Thank you," Anna said to her boss's retreating back.

But it wasn't until Jemima had disappeared down the hallway that Anna felt the real weight of what had happened. Because it had *actually happened.*

Jemima had opened the door to Anna potentially having an exhibit of her own. Finally.

This called for lunch. A celebration lunch of sushi, of course. She grabbed her coat, scarf, hat, purse, and headed out into the cold December weather. Her favorite sushi spot wasn't far from the museum, but still far enough away that she had to bundle up.

A block away from the museum, on the opposite side of the street, was the Grove Hotel. Their famous dreidel display was scheduled to go up within the next few weeks, and she couldn't help but head closer to sneak a peek at the window...

Only as she crossed the street, she saw a familiar figure, in a long, black coat, his brown hair flying.

Jacob.

Jacob Horowitz-Margareten.

Her first love. Her childhood best friend. Her most recent ex.

She hadn't seen him since their last breakup a year ago in October. Their third. The same song, different verse—another missed relationship commitment (whether it was his or hers) and a text message, an echo of the previous breakup three years before that, and their first back in college. Since then, she'd managed to avoid Rockliffe Manor, the town, and Rockliffe, his family's home, very successfully.

What was he doing *here now?*

Did she want to say hello?

Did she have to say hello?

All she knew was that he looked lost, and it wasn't just the cold. His skin looked paler than usual, his normally bright blue eyes looked flat.

Her heart pounded against her chest as she got closer. He was...

He was so much. He filled her vision and her memory, taking up the space she thought she'd successfully banished him from forever in one fell swoop.

She had to say hello. It was their rule. "Jacob?"

Manhattan had a different rhythm from Rockliffe Manor, especially in early December. Faster, probably because it ran at its own pace as opposed to figuring out how to handle everybody else's.

At least that was how Jacob Horowitz-Margareten saw it.

Early December was even more difficult. Triple-breasted suits and heavy coats reminded him of photos his ancestors had taken. The weight of that legacy always lay heavily on his shoulders, but this felt worse.

He'd have one fast meeting with the Brady Group, a group of investors he despised enough to inform them in person that he wanted nothing to do with them. He'd already fired the advisor who suggested working with them in the first place, something Jacob should have done months, if not years, ago.

Guilt was strong, but not stronger than his desire to work with people who didn't take advantage of others. Not to mention, the list he'd received two years before from his father's estate attorney had indicated the former investment advisor was to be given only one chance to prove himself, and this was it. Predictably, the man had failed. Jacob had also gotten really sick of the many times the advisor had suggested he move his accounts offshore "to avoid tax consequences." There were only so many times he could say "not in this lifetime or the next. I believe in paying taxes."

After Jacob personally helped introduce this set of aristocratic garbage to consequences and the SEC, he'd be done. He'd be free.

He could do something better with his time.

Like call his assistant and be on a flight to Texas within the next two hours. There he'd be able to observe the mobile office he'd set up down by the border. Making sure the staff was doing its job, acting as a helping hand.

His goal had always been to make sure organizations like the Jewish Immigrant Defense Society, and others that worked to help those caught in the net of governmental immigration and family separation policies, never had to go without anything. Ever. So that they could do their jobs protecting and advocating for the most vulnerable without focusing on the basics: rent, phone bills, office supplies.

"Jacob."

Christopher Hayward.

Jacob didn't want anything more to do with Brady; they'd not only taken money from Hayward but had also recruited him as the public face of this zero-interest grant campaign. Hayward was scum, smarm, slime, not even fit for shoe leather. He was dangerous, with an extensive list of arrests and charges stemming from the way he treated women and those who he believed "lesser." Each of those charges had been dismissed, his record cleansed, contributing to the man's mistaken belief that he'd never face consequences for anything he'd done.

He would learn otherwise.

But instead of letting any of that slip through his mask, Jacob turned and nodded. Christopher Hayward had waxy hair, the clear red undertones in his skin that smelled of alcohol even if his breath didn't.

"Yes. Christopher. Hello."

"Listen," Hayward said. "We have a room inside, just waiting for you and…"

From the corner of his eye, he saw a figure moving quickly through the streets of Manhattan. Sure, agile, and familiar as the gloves he was wearing. His heart pounded.

Anna Cohen.

He did *not* want Christopher Hayward to notice Anna in any way, for any reason. He couldn't be trusted, not only because Hayward had a record that didn't stick, but the idea of showing Hayward that Anna was someone important to him made him physically sick.

The only thing that would save him was the messy end to their last attempt at a relationship. All he could do was hope she wouldn't decide it was time to approach him, and if she did, hope his mask held. Because he'd been many things in his life, but indifferent to Anna was never one of them.

She crossed the street, and as Hayward continued to yammer on about the interior of the restaurant where the meeting was to take place, his heart started to pound.

"Jacob?"

The sound of her voice caressed his eardrums. He thought of ice, the fjords of Norway, anything cold enough to chill his blood. He still noticed her bright brown eyes and the way her pale skin was turned bright by the cold. He managed a slight lift of an eyebrow, almost as if he were looking at her through a quizzing glass.

"Jacob?"

The clear upset in her tone shouldn't hurt. He was ice, glass, frozen. Doing his best to make dammed sure the ticking time bomb standing to his right didn't take an interest.

"Yes?"

A heartbeat of silence. Two, three.

He tried not to look too closely at Anna's expression, at the lip she bit, the quick movements of her eyelashes. He was ice, unyielding, unbending.

"Never mind."

Four. Five.

Only when she turned her back on him and walked away could he breathe again. It broke him, but it was over.

She was gone.

Thankfully, Hayward didn't say anything. To him, Anna hadn't even been important enough to grace the bottoms of his shoes.

The meeting lasted only two minutes, the amount of time it took for Jacob to denounce their scheme and watch the SEC agent he'd alerted shake hands with the gang and start his grilling.

Jacob had his car stop off at Abe's Kitchen to get a quick sandwich for the ride back; a soda and a sandwich on rye was what he needed to get deep into his skin again.

There was much to do anyway. Paperwork back at the house. Scheduling for the next few days, and a Texas trip in the next twenty-four hours.

Hanukkah, New Year.

Calendars and appointments and organizing and...

No time.

Only later did he let himself break. Only later did he think about the expression on Anna's face as she walked away. Only later did he think about the consequences of what he'd done.

He'd broken their rule, the one rule between them. The one that had lasted through friendships and attempted relationships, beginnings and endings and summers.

Years of history, the most important relationship in his life.

Gone.

And there was absolutely nothing in the world he could do to fix it.

Chapter Two

Five months later.

JACOB HOROWITZ-MARGARETEN WAS exhausted.

His flight from Texas had gotten in later than planned, which meant a half-awake conversation with the driver ended up with him here, at Rockliffe, and not in the city. But his alarm was going off, and he couldn't shut it down because he was tired. The fund needed watching, the grantees needed questions answered, the new round of applicants for grants needed review, and all of them needed him.

This was what happened when you went five months without an investment manager. But he didn't work with people who didn't share his values. And he'd take the same action again when he was confronted with the same questions and similar evidence at any time in the future.

So much to do.

There were also the last two items on the list he'd gotten from his father's estate attorney—only one open task, one more left in an envelope he kept in a desk drawer.

Make it better, Jacob, the letter accompanying the items

had said. *You've always been a better person than I was, so you can make these things right. You're the only one who can.*

Sometimes the list weighed on him; the responsibility of posthumously fixing his father's mistakes as he tried to keep from making his own was a large one. But it was his legacy.

Unfortunately, his concentration was broken by a buzzing noise. He picked up his phone only to discover a blinking light, indicating a message had come into the Foundation email. A quick switch into that inbox showed him yet another request for archives access from the Manhattan Museum of Jewish History and its head curator, Jemima Kellerman.

Her pretense of civility sent shudders down his spine, even half asleep. He grabbed a sweatshirt, pulled it on, and headed into the downstairs study.

His slippers slushed and slid on the tile as he headed into the office, past the photographs of generations of his ancestors. It was warm—carpet, bookcases, and bright lights. He pulled the shades down because light before caffeine made his head pound.

As his computer booted up, he turned around and shoved a pod into the single-cup coffeemaker he kept in this office. A slight knock made him turn around briefly, only to see his mother. She looked well; the olive undertones in her skin were bright. He turned his attention back to his coffee.

"Morning," he managed.

"So I've been in touch with the Historical Society."

Historical Society?

Ah, right. The only one his mother loved speaking to, volunteering at, and championing was the Rockliffe Manor one. "Oh?"

"Yes. They need a new project, not to mention the Chamber of Commerce has been sniffing around about our participation in Summer Days and a few other things."

"Speaking of sniffing." He ran a hand through his hair. "The foundation, or you, got another request from Jemima Kellerman at the Manhattan Museum of Jewish History. You should turn them down again."

"Why?" His mother put her coffee cup down on the desk, took a seat, her green eyes focusing on him like an electron microscope. He wasn't sure what she was looking for, but he was pretty well aware she was going to find nothing before he'd had caffeine of his own.

"Because I don't want Jemima Kellerman and her reputation for destroying priceless family heirlooms anywhere near the archives."

It took his mother a moment to register the words, but she nodded. "Fair enough. But you know who works there with her, right?"

He knew. But only because he'd looked her up in a late night search fueled by the desire to know. That glimpse he'd seen of her back in December made him weirdly nostalgic.

But he would never do anything about it. Anna's life and work were hers, not his. She'd made it clear where they stood even before that glimpse in December, and lingering, misplaced feelings about her or mistrust of her boss weren't enough for him to cross that line. Nothing was. But instead of telling his mother all of this, he went for something else. "I've been desperately trying to forget."

His mother looked at him. "Mm-hmm."

Once again he didn't know what bit of information his mother wished to glean from his expression.

"Yes?"

She shook her head. "But yes. I'll deny the museum again, and then speak to the Historical Society…"

"Historical Society?" He knew there was a point to this line of conversation; she'd mentioned the society twice now. He just hadn't figured it out yet.

"Summer Days, Jacob. I think we should tell the story of our family. Some of it at least, because I think we can use this year's theme as a test run for the historical wing, open it and see what happens."

Aaaah.

Over the years, the family had moved out of the part of the mansion they called "the historical wing." It was too historic to change, too important to live in. They'd maintained it, of course, and at some point, some relative had begun the process of opening it up to the public but had never quite managed to do it. It had become an albatross of a project. "You can't do it on your own," he replied.

"Of course not," his mother replied, indignant. "What

do you take me for? This would be a project, and we would need help to complete it in time for Summer Days. And that, my dear boy, is where the Rockliffe Manor Historical Society comes in."

He nodded as he looked through some spreadsheets the head of the Rockliffe Manor Chamber of Commerce had sent him. A few of the stores needed some help, and as he'd expected, one of them was just below the mark. He needed to pop in and see what was going on, find out what kind of help the owner might need. "Yeah," he said, already distract-ed.

"Good. Glad to hear you agree with this idea."

He pulled back down to earth quickly. "What idea?"

His mother wore an indulgent smile. He'd missed some-thing with all of the details and the data that had already lodged themselves in his brain. "Asking the Historical Society for help with the opening of the historical wing in time for Summer Days, as well as some investigation of the archives. Maybe throwing—"

"Definitely a stipend. Because you're not going to get someone to do this without taking care of their time as well as their expertise."

His mother's nod was not indulgent this time. There was pride in her eyes. And that made him feel just a little better.

ANNA COHEN WAS ready. Revitalized by the Passover break, fueled by her dreams. She wanted to put stories of Jews who used their voices, and spoke out against those who abused their power, on the walls of the Manhattan Museum of Jewish History and she knew she could do it. Only one obstacle stood in her way.

Jemima Kellerman. Her boss. Who was an enigma if nothing else.

After that glimpse of praise, excitement, and approval back in December, Jemima hadn't accepted any of the ideas Anna had put forward. Even worse, she hadn't even given any sign of why none of the previous ideas had worked.

No critique, no criticism, no insight into what Jemima was looking for. Which was disappointing, if not entirely unexpected. Jemima wasn't good at guidance, after all. She was good at working with donors but not so much at teaching the business and guiding principles of curation.

But this exhibit was important; the timing was important. Anna had to make sure she said the right words because she needed to convince Jemima that *this* was the time for this exhibit. Not tomorrow. Not next year. Now.

To that end, she picked up the papers she'd worked on over the holiday with her friends back in Hollowville, and put them in the portfolio her best friend Sarah had given her as a gift before checking the time.

9:55 a.m.

Five minutes to get to Jemima's office.

Her quick steps clicked against the floor of the museum. And as she arrived at her boss's office, Jemima opened the door with a flourish that almost knocked Anna over.

"Anna, darling," she said, beckoning her into the office. "Come in, come in."

Right on time, open, and gracious but yet just a tad held back. Anna pulled her lips into a professional smile. She could do this. "Thank you," she said, following Jemima into a lushly carpeted office that looked just a bit off. Yes, there were the right elements, the right books, the right…

"Anna," Jemima said, gesturing toward a chair, showing off her French manicure. "I hope you had a wonderful holiday. Now I have loads to do today with the new exhibit and all, but I remember you wanted to talk to me about something?"

"Yes!" Anna sat down on the chair Jemima had designated. "I actually want to talk to you about an exhibit I'd like to put in the open space in the museum starting in September."

"Right. After my Gilded Age Jewry exhibit." Jemima beamed. "How are the cards going?"

"Well, we're getting close to the end of the material—"

"Right. Right. Now what were you talking about?"

Anna took a breath. This was it. "So one of the things I love about your exhibit," she began, "is that it centers on the areas of Gilded Age history that really aren't discussed outside of our circles."

"Yes." Jemima beamed. "These families were grand and

gorgeous and wonderful, but nobody wants to talk about them because it makes them feel better to see us as not so grand."

Which was the truth. And now she had to be careful with her words. "They also have such a rich history of social action. And it's driven by an inherent legacy and—"

Her boss raised a well-curved eyebrow. "Social action, hmm? Social justice?"

She nodded and tried not to bristle at the derisive tone. "They do. We have a rich history of both of those things as a community. These days it's important to emphasize this aspect of our culture."

Jemima bit her lip, her expression dubious, as her gaze landed on the pile of notes in Anna's lap. "Let me see that."

Jemima took the offered notes in a way that showed off that French manicure again. Oddly enough, the white on the tip of her boss's nails matched the printed sheet of her outline.

Seconds passed as Anna tried to glean something from Jemima's expression. This was the moment of truth.

"Very, very interesting," Jemima murmured as she flipped through the notes. After a few moments, she looked up, her brown eyes meeting Anna's. "You know," she said, "there are some prize pieces I'm missing for the exhibit."

Now it was Anna's turn to bite her lip. "I'm not following."

"I figure it's an interesting little thing." Jemima waved a

hand. "You've been asking for more responsibility, and you've put together this great exhibit outline."

This was good. This was really good. This time she'd managed to write the right words. And yet…something felt off.

"But you understand that putting an exhibit together means getting in touch with primary source holders, right?"

"Yes," she replied, hoping she'd covered that information in her outline. She'd had conversations with Batya about contacts with museums in California. "I have—"

"You have phone numbers and contacts, and I love that. But I need to see if you can actually *get* anything from these people. Which means I have a task for you, and it goes quite well with the rather large hole in my Gilded Age exhibit."

Anna nodded. "Yes?"

"One of the families is refusing to give me anything from their archives, much less speak to me. Everybody else has been wonderful, museums and the sort. But these people…" Jemima visibly shuddered. "Anyway, if you can approach them, gain access to their archives, and fill the hole in my collection, you can have the exhibit space after this exhibit ends."

"Who?" But there was a feeling deep in her gut telling her she already knew. Who else would be so extremely particular about anything?

Her mind raced back to December, just before Hanukkah and a walk she'd taken on her lunch break. The last time she'd seen him.

"The Horowitz-Margareten family. They live on Long Island, at Rockliff—"

"Rockliffe Manor," she replied. As if she could forget. But all she said was: "Yes."

"Good. Contact them and see if you can get me something."

Anna tried to keep her composure as the pause lasted too long. The idea of following her boss's instructions when they were couched in the undertone of personal gain left her nauseated.

"You know. For the exhibit."

As Anna left the office, having been summarily dismissed, the sinking feeling in her stomach fell to her toes. She was in serious trouble, and she had no idea what to do about it. Unfortunately, she couldn't figure out how to fix the problem in time for lunch.

She decided to drown her sorrows in sushi.

Sorrows. Which meant all of the memories of Rockliffe Manor, going back to her childhood.

The person she'd managed to avoid and not think about since December.

Jacob Horowitz-Margareten.

Her first love, her...was there even a word big enough to describe their relationship? Two against the world, the one person she'd always been sure of despite the wild impossibility of their circumstances. Even after they ceased to be a couple and lost touch.

Until he broke their rule five months before.

It hurt more than she could think about most days, which is probably why she spent most of the time *not* thinking about it. Or him.

And now she needed to get into his family archives.

Fate hated her.

How was she going to get the information she needed without dealing with him, with his family, directly?

Could she?

That was the question.

As she dipped her tuna rolls in a mix of soy sauce and wasabi, she remembered the first time she'd had sushi. On a lunch break with one of her mentors, Dr. Beatrice Humphries.

The woman who had run the Rockliffe Manor Historical Society with an iron fist wrapped in a velvet glove for as long as Anna could remember. The woman who had given her a summer job, a place to study, and most importantly, Dr. Humphries had taught her how to tell stories. If *anybody* could help her get into the Horowitz-Margareten archives without dealing with the family, it would be her. Anna called the Rockliffe Manor Historical Society as soon as she got back from lunch.

"Anna," the woman on the other end of the phone bubbled in a voice Anna would know with her eyes closed. "How are you, darling?"

"Hi, Dr. Humphries," she said, barely able to hide her excitement at the sound of the other woman's voice. "I'm good. Glad to hear your voice. I'm actually coming down this weekend, and I'd love to take a look at some of the documents and things you have in the society's archives."

"Oh that's wonderful," Dr. H said. "It's so fortuitous you called."

"Why?"

"Well, a project has come up. If you're already coming down to do some research, I'd love to see you at least contend for it. It's not a direct project, of course."

"Oh?" Not a direct project was code for something the Historical Society partnered on but didn't administer completely. "Sounds good," she said as she made a note in her planner.

"It's something about the archives. Ours and the Horowitz-Margaretens' archives."

Even better. "Really?" Maybe fate didn't hate her so much. "Sure."

"Good to hear. I'll tell Rose you're interested."

There was only one Rose anybody in Rockliffe Manor spoke about in that manner or with that tone.

Rose Horowitz-Margareten.

Jacob's mother. As long as she'd known him, she'd known Rose. Sometimes she was kind, sometimes she was rude, but she was omnipresent in Rockliffe Manor.

She swallowed a sigh, because, of course, there were never easy days.

But this project was important enough that she had to pull herself together. "Thank you," she managed.

Dr. Humphries didn't answer instantly, which was fine. What could be a problem was the rapid click of keys in the background followed by a beep, indicating the older woman was sending an email. "And now we wait. So tell me," she said. "How are you otherwise, Anna? How is the MMJH treating you?"

And as Anna began to tell her mentor about the excitement of working at the museum, there was a second beep.

"Sorry to interrupt, my dear, but it looks like Rose is excited that you might be interested in the project and wants to talk to you."

"In—?"

"Hold on." There was fumbling and the click of keys. "Rose is going to call you."

"Call…me?"

"In the next few minutes. She wants to talk to you. Wants to see you, but I suspect she'll settle for a phone call, because I've given her your number at the museum."

As she started to consider the implications, her phone beeped. A slow readout showed a 516 area code, and a number that sat as a ghost in her memory.

"That's her on my other line."

"Oh good. I'll hang up, and you and she can discuss details."

And just like that, she ended one call, held her breath, and composed herself before she answered the next.

"Hello. Anna Cohen speaking."

"Anna, love, this is Rose."

The other woman didn't have to say her last name. Anna knew exactly who she was. The love was new. "Hello, Mrs.—"

"Rose," she repeated. "You grew up at my knee, child. You call me Mrs. anything and I'll feel rather ancient."

"Rose, then. I assume you're calling about the project associated with the Historical Society and the archives?"

"You have the most convenient timing," Rose replied, seemingly oblivious to how much the world worked around her whims and desires. "I left a message with Beatrice, and I just got her email. We'd had a lovely tea earlier and spoke about a project very near and dear to my heart."

Anna bit her lip. Hard.

"There is a wing of the house that various Horowitz-Margaretens have slowly attempted to open to the public for years. Nobody's managed it, but I've had enough of this waiting. Anyway, it isn't a thing my family can manage on our own, and so I've reached out to the Historical Society for help. It would be a temporary project, of course, and it would come with both a stipend and concurrent access to the archives."

She couldn't help the sharp intake of breath.

"Access to the archives would be granted on a temporary

basis for this project. However, when it's over, the curator of the exhibit would possibly be afforded lengthier access to the archives for other outside projects, based on the circumstances and the need."

Outside projects. Like Jemima's. Like hers about social justice.

This could work. Which meant she needed more information. "Aside from the opening, what's the focus of the project? The deadline?"

"Ah. There's my professional curator. Excellent." There was a pause. "So, I'm looking for an exhibit, using the material from the archives, to be displayed in the wing when it opens in time for the town's Summer Days festival."

Anna had absolutely no idea what that was, but she could figure it out. She had enough people she could ask, after all. "Okay. So curation in conjunction with the festival."

"Good. Now if you take the job—you would be my ideal candidate—as I said, there would be a stipend to compensate you for your time. Your expertise doesn't come cheap, especially since in order to take on the project, you'll have to take time off from your job, hmm?"

"I'll speak to my boss and see what kind of arrangement can be made. If she gives me the okay, then I'll be there this weekend to possibly talk further on Monday?"

"I suspect"—there might have been a snort on the other end of the phone, but Anna could not have been certain—

"that she might not have a problem with any arrangement we make, considering she has attempted to get into our archives numerous times."

Anna paused. "I'll contact you as soon as I finish speaking to her."

As she ended the conversation, she typed up a quick request for time off and a proposal to show Jemima and left the office. Things were moving quickly, and despite her concerns about being in Rockliffe Manor again, she was excited.

THE LAST GASP of Spring wrapped around Jacob, seeped into his bones. He could have done this over the phone, for sure, but he needed to see his friend.

In person.

Which is probably why Tony Liu had turned this into an in-person meeting, down at the bar overlooking the space that would soon become the town's famous outdoor café. "Drinks on me," Jacob said as he sat down. "What are you having?"

"Apparently, a taste of your humble pie."

Jacob sighed. His friend's brown eyes were bright; he was having way too much fun with this. And he could see the pink undertones in his friend's skin. "Yeah. Why I thought waiting for five months to ask you to manage my investments was a good idea, I'll never know."

"Because you were taking pity on my workload?"

"Probably. I won't make that mistake again."

"Yeah. Who actually thought that an 'investment opportunity' with a team that included Christopher Hayward as a silent partner would be something you'd be interested in?"

"Nobody with actual insight, that's for sure. Speaking of which, I wonder how Hayward is enjoying what the SEC is dishing out his way."

"Probably as much as you enjoyed working with your father's investment manager."

Jacob nodded. "So very true."

"How is that list going, by the way? Did you check to see what was going on with Smith's Dry Cleaners?"

"Turns out," Jacob told his friend as he went into his notes app to find the notes he'd taken during the meeting, "that they need more help. So what do you think about widening the parameters of the program to include extra childcare and maybe a jobs training program?"

"I like that idea. First generation small-business owners need more help in a lot of ways, and we're providing that."

"Notice you're finally saying *we*? How long did that take you?"

"Fine," Tony said, his tone a weird mix of reluctance and excitement. "So part of the reason I love working with you, dude, is that we do this Mitzvah Alliance program. And yes, fine. I'm finally talking partnership."

Jacob reached into the folder he'd brought. "Look over the papers, my friend," he said, passing over the partnership agreement. "I want papers and signatures because those never lie."

"These papers and the investment papers. Got it. So much paperwork. Speaking of papers, there's a rumor they're opening Rockliffe to some kind of tourism?"

"Yeah. No rumor. The wing—the part of the house nobody's used for years, the one we kept as close as possible to original—is going to be open for Summer Days. And maybe after, depending on how the trial period goes. The Foundation is hiring a curator to create an exhibit."

"Good," Tony replied. "Impressive. And the curator?"

"Interview on Monday. One candidate. Foundation's taking care of it, which means I'm not involved."

Tony raised an eyebrow. Had he answered too quickly for his friend? Too flippantly?

"What? You mean you're not interested that your mother, through the foundation, is hiring a curator to create an exhibit in the house you grew up in and partially live in? Or is there something you're not telling me?"

Tony was from New Jersey, so his friend didn't know the history or the stories that fueled the town's gossip mill. "Not interested," he said, finally. "I don't need to deal with all the aspects of the foundation, as well as the list, as well as the investments, as well as the alliance."

"This sounds like you're listening to advice, but..." Tony

paused. Reading between the lines was one of his friend's strengths, and the very last thing Jacob wanted was to explain why he wasn't interested in dealing with or interfering with the lives and careers of curators. "I don't actually believe it."

He shrugged. "That's okay. I am excited that you're finally signing partnership papers."

"I will also point out that despite the fact that some kind of economic development commission was on your father's list, you haven't seemed this excited about anything since that class on impact investment in college."

Jacob smiled. "I hadn't expected to learn about impact investment in a classroom."

And as they settled into conversation, he realized how lucky he was to have friends like Tony. Things were changing, whether or not he was ready for them to. And it was especially important to keep his friends close.

INSTEAD OF TELLING Sarah and Batya in an email or a video chat or a phone call that she was going to be temporarily moving to Rockliffe Manor, Anna invited her two best friends over to her apartment for dinner to tell them in person.

"So," she said, turning in Sarah's direction after dessert, "you're moving, right? You're going to leave Hollowville?"

Predictably, Sarah shook her head. "Nope. Isaac and I are

splitting time between Hollowville and his place because we like both and why should we decide?"

Anna nodded, feeling better about the way this discussion was going.

"For now?"

"For now," Sarah confirmed, suspicion in her green eyes.

"And you"—she turned to Batya—"what's your story?"

"Website design is the best," her friend replied, sliding her way into the question, pushing her glasses up as she sat back against her chair. "I like it much better. I think the Historical Society is fun, but they don't have the money to pay me for full-time work. So it's very much in flux. My life, I mean."

"Which means that when I say I'm going to Rockliffe Manor temporarily, I would very much like the both of you, with your lives in flux, to believe me."

Her statement was followed by silence. What did that mean?

"What are you going to be doing in Rockliffe Manor, exactly?" Sarah asked.

"The town has something called Summer Days. And the Historical Society, as well as a whole bunch of other societies, have booths celebrating each year's theme."

"And your specific job?"

Anna sighed. Sarah was on a mission; there were details and subtexts her friend thought she saw. Which meant she had to be specific. "My boss wants me to speak to one of the families that live in town about donating some items from their archives to the museum's collection as well as the newest exhibit she's working on. In exchange for me obtaining the materials, she's giving me the time off to work on the collection for the Historical Society but more importantly, my own exhibit on Jewish social justice issues at the museum after the Gilded Age exhibit comes down."

"Which is great," Batya said. "I love this for you."

She did too. More responsibility and on site archival work. So many things she loved.

"So?" Sarah asked in a way that meant trouble. "Whose family archives are you working with?"

She braced herself. "The Horowitz-Margareten family."

"And you're okay with...Jacob?"

"Jacob has nothing to do with this."

"Who is Jacob?"

Anna sighed. Sometimes it was hard to believe she'd been friendly with Batya for only five months. Other times, like now, it was easier. "Call him my past," Anna replied as pleasantly but as decisively as she could. "Also call him someone who has nothing to do with my present."

Sarah leaned back against the wall, and the smug expression on her face made Anna want to yell. But Sarah didn't say a word, apparently wanting to let the expression speak for itself.

"You're working with his family history," Batya pointed out. "He's got to be involved in some capacity, right?"

Anna shook her head as Sarah snickered in the background. "You're mistaking this. You know about the Carnegies and the Vanderbilts and the Rockefellers, the people most Americans think populated the Gilded Age, right?"

"Yeah." Batya shook her head. "I also know that they weren't the only ones. So much gets selectively excised from discussion and erased from the history books."

"Yes. Exactly," Anna replied, easily falling into the narrative. "So the Gilded Age histories are also usually told through a Christian-centric cultural lens. Exhibits and discussions rarely focus on those who don't fit into the prescribed narrative."

"Except the Truitts, of course," Batya interjected, grinning. "Because you know they're fascinating. But speaking of fascinating, what's the story of Jacob and his family?"

"Yes," Sarah said, grinning. "Tell us, Anna. What *is* the story of Jacob and his family?"

"So from a professional standpoint," Anna replied, ignoring the undertone in Sarah's voice, "people do know some good details on the history of the Horowitz-Margareten family, like the middle finger one of his ancestors gave to a Long Island town when they built Rockliffe, their ancestral house, as well as the general details of the fight that precipitated the incorporation of the town of Rockliffe Manor around it later. Which means the archives are, like, practically undiscovered territory. And I get to dive into them."

"Unexamined because they're private and want to stay out of the history books, or is there another reason?"

Batya was a sharp cookie—not that Anna didn't know that, but it was becoming clearer the longer she spent with the other woman. "My guess is, a lot of historians didn't want to confront the anti-Semitism necessary to tell the Horowitz-Margaretens' story. You know? You go two seconds in and there you have them openly confronting anti-Semitism as they work to make the world better without a buffer. It's…they've always been a lot."

"Okay." Batya laughed. "So you dated, like, American Jewish royalty?"

"He's not like that," Anna said. "But we share emotional baggage I have no use for anymore."

Sarah raised an eyebrow. "So what are you doing for this festival?"

"I'm going to be curating an exhibit for the wing of the house the family is opening in conjunction with the town's Summer Days festival."

"Which means you're going to be working in Jacob's house, right?"

"For the festival, yes. Not with him. I mean, he doesn't live there, not really, I don't think. I mean, I know he has a place in the city. At least he won't be in the wing I'll be working in."

"I don't believe you," Sarah said. "But I guess you'll have to figure this out on your own, hmm?"

"Meanwhile, on a complete side note," Batya interjected, "do they need a web designer? Also do you want someone to watch your apartment?"

Aaaah, Batya, her knight in shining armor. "First, the website. Are you talking about the family or the festival?"

"For the festival," Batya replied. "Though I wouldn't mind working on a website for the new museum."

"I'll see what I can do. Either my grandmother or my contact at the Historical Society will know who's running the festival and can ask them. The festival committee will probably appreciate the help."

"Especially if their festival website was as horrible as the one the—"

"Don't say it," Sarah warned. "Don't say it. You fixed the Hanukkah festival website. It's yours now."

Anna grinned as Batya threw up a hand. "Fine, fine, fine. So I'll wait to hear from you, and then I'll contact whoever you tell me to."

Anna nodded, but as she did, realized she hadn't actually answered Batya's second question. "And I would love if someone watched my place, especially if that someone was trustworthy."

Batya beamed. "That would be me."

"That makes me feel better," Anna said, relieved a piece of the puzzle she hadn't even considered had fallen into place. "Stay over; I'll give you keys as I'm leaving."

"I can't believe you're actually going to leave tomorrow

morning," Sarah said.

"My God." Anna filled her water glass. "Stop being dramatic. It's not like it's far to Rockliffe Manor, and it's not like I'm living there permanently."

"Yeah, well," Sarah replied, taking a cookie from the plate and heading to the door. "I am excited for you, but you need to give me time to adjust."

"What is this need for adjustment?" Anna asked.

"Not geographically, but you're going to be delving into your past with Jacob as well as his family's." Sarah replied.

Anna shook her head at her friend. "Just because you have your happy ending."

"Hold your horses. I'm not talking about a happy ending," her best friend returned. "I just hope you get closure. What do they say about history?"

"Only that people who don't know it are doomed to repeat it. And I, thankfully, am not doomed."

Sarah blew Anna a kiss and closed the door behind her.

"Not doomed, huh?"

Anna shook her head as she turned to Batya. "Nope. I'm ready. Life is giving me a chance to change my story, and I am grabbing hold of it."

Batya nodded. "I know that all too well," she replied. "I hope you can get the ending you want."

"I do, too," Anna replied.

"Have you decided what ending you want though?"

"The triumphant curator opening a brand new exhibit,

of course. Now come on, let me show you a few things, give you some notes." Because her friend's life was going to change in the morning, too.

Chapter Three

ANNA LEFT BROOKLYN after the morning rush hour, the drive to Rockliffe Manor was uneventful and there wasn't much traffic to meet her when she arrived in town, Which made it easier to linger, so she drove a little slower in an attempt to catch a glimpse of what made Rockliffe Manor tick now.

At least that's what she called attempting to shove the town out of the space it had occupied in her memory and into her present; with her window down, she could focus on the smells, the new construction in place of old memories, new signs in place of old ones. Nostalgia wasn't going to help anybody, which was a strange line in the sand to draw, especially when doing her job right meant diving into history for its own sake.

That put her on her grandmother's front porch just in time for lunch—and Anna's grandmother had prepared a great one.

"Yes," Oma said as they were clearing the lunch dishes. "The Manor has really changed a great deal since you last spent quality time here. You should go and see it. I think they're about to start setting up the outdoor café, but the rest of it is absolutely worth seeing. They've made a lot of changes here. Good ones."

"It's a good idea," Anna replied. "Is there anything you need while I'm in town?"

"Yes," Oma returned, her hazel eyes bright with a plan. "I do need a challah for dinner."

Mission in hand, Anna headed upstairs to change into her armor: a cute skirt, blouse and cardigan, as if she were going to work at the museum. If nothing else, that would remind her that she was a professional and not a stressed-out, overly emotional…whatever she was.

She also brought her museum ID. Even if the reference librarian at the Rockliffe Manor Library didn't know who she was, they'd recognize her badge.

Inevitably, she ended up in the deep basement archives of the library, a welcoming place where the books had yellowing pages, signs of history transcribed on the page. After grabbing a few titles, she checked them out and walked back into the streets of town. It wasn't home, of course, wasn't Brooklyn or Hollowville, but it felt comfortable; the smells and sounds of the most important parts of her childhood.

Of course, it was still early on a Friday afternoon, and the streets were starting to get pretty busy. The weather had started to change, and people were in the process of setting up the outdoor café at the center of the business district. She wasn't going to spend the afternoon watching the setup, so she continued to meander around, stopping in front of a bakery. The sign was bright, with a logo and lettering that looked somewhat familiar for reasons she was having trouble placing. But the vanilla-scented cloud of pastry cream that hit her nose as she opened the door confirmed she'd made the right decision.

"Oh wow," she managed.

The woman behind the counter met her with sparkling brown, close set eyes. "Best reaction I've had all day. What can I get you?"

"What's your favorite?"

The woman, who was starting to look very familiar, gestured across the counter, the cool highlights of her pale skin bright against the light of the bakery. "This is a passion project, so I love it all. I don't have to bake what I don't want to, and I get to have fun with flavors."

Anna nodded. "I love that so much. I totally get that. So you pick," she said. "No important allergies to think about, so I'd like one of what makes you happiest to see."

"I think we're going to be friends. I'm Charlotte Liu."

She shook Charlotte's outstretched hand over the counter. "Anna Cohen."

But there was something familiar about Charlotte, something about her smile.

Wait.

She'd read an article about a young chef and budding

entrepreneur who had three restaurants. One in Brooklyn, not far from Isaac's place. One in Manhattan, not far from the museum. And rumors of a pastry shop and restaurant outside the city.

Here.

Oh wow.

"Of C'shop in Brooklyn?"

"And C's Place here, yes." Charlotte beamed as she reached across the counter with a flourish, a waxed paper package in her hand. "I've been here more often recently because I'm preparing the place for Summer Days and the influx of people that comes with summer."

Anna nodded. "I totally get that. I'm back in town mostly to help with Summer Days and a few other things."

"So what do you do when you're not here in Rockliffe Manor?"

"I'm an assistant curator at the Manhattan Museum of Jewish History."

"Right." As Anna took a bite into the flaky, amazingly soft pastry Charlotte snapped her fingers. "Wait. You're here for the exhibit at Rockliffe? Working with Rose on the wing?"

"I…" She paused once again. Gossip and conversation spread quickly through this small town. "Yes," she said. "I might be."

"Sorry. Chamber of Commerce conversations and, you know, the small-town gossip chain. But why do you think you won't?"

"I have a meeting on Monday that will confirm what I'm doing. Either I'll be working on the wing or with Dr. Humphries at the Historical Society."

"I adore Dr. Humphries. I will adore her more if she gives me insight into her special tea blend." Charlotte shook her head. "I've been trying to get that information from her forever."

"She's pretty attached to it," Anna replied. "It's her pride and joy, you know?"

"It is. And I do, all too well."

But the response wasn't words; it was a creaking noise, then the swooshing sound of a door shoved open and closed. Anna tried to see better as the footsteps on the tile got louder.

Who was that?

Charlotte turned toward the door. "You look like a snowman," she said to the person.

Jacob?

JACOB HAD DISCOVERED the joys of folding dough. Whether he was making bourekas, or hamantaschen, or rugelach, or kreplach, or any of their other international cousins, it was soothing.

"Just don't destroy my kitchen," Charlotte Liu had ordered as she headed back to the front. "I've got everything shipshape for when everybody comes back tomorrow."

He didn't laugh. Charlotte was serious about her kitchens; she didn't become a world-renowned chef and restaurateur without caring. Of course, why she'd indulged him and taught him to fold the dough in the first place was beyond him. Probably because she'd had enough of him beating Tony, her husband, at cards. Either way, he'd been grateful.

"I'll be careful."

As the sound of Charlotte's footsteps got softer, indicating she'd pushed open the door and moved to the front counter, he turned on the music in his headphones and returned to folding. She'd given him instructions, half out of pity and half out of amusement. She undoubtedly hadn't expected he'd complete them, but he'd do his best. This was complex.

Which meant he had to clear his head completely, lose himself in the patterns of dough as it came together into something special—at least that was the theory. It was so much easier to confront dough than any of the other things creating difficulties in his life.

But too soon he was done, the tray full of pastries, his hands covered in flour and powdered sugar. He turned off the music and pushed open the door that separated the kitchen from the front of the store.

Charlotte was talking to someone.

Not just *someone.*

Anna.

Her voice wrapped around him like a cotton blanket; he'd know it anywhere.

In town. In the city. On the phone. In person.

He could barely breathe, and she looked as if she'd been frozen.

"What were you up to in there?" Charlotte said as she met his eyes.

"Uh," he managed, having trouble remembering how to speak. "Hi. Excuse me."

"I…"

"There's no excuse for him," Charlotte interjected, looking at him as if he was a wayward preschooler. Which, for all intents and purposes, he was. Especially as Anna stood there, as icy as he'd felt five months before.

"And," Charlotte continued, turning toward Anna before turning back to him as she graciously attempted to bridge the mile-wide conversation gap, "I take it you two know each other?"

Jacob watched the anger flit across Anna's face before her mask of politeness settled. He wanted to burst out of the bakery and leave Anna to her own devices and her own life, but he couldn't. All he could do was nod.

"Safe to say," Anna replied, "that's the case."

There were other words she clearly wanted to say, but for no reason he could think of, she didn't. He could barely remember his own name; all he could think of was hers. "Anna—"

"Now, Jacob? Really?"

He shook his head, swallowed back words neither of them was ready to hear. "No. Not now. But it is good to see you." Instead of waiting for another response from Anna, he turned to Charlotte. "I'll see you later?"

"You're leaving. Just like that?"

He nodded. Because he couldn't stay. The ocean of regret, hurt, and all of the other stray emotions tied up in a lifetime of knowing Anna threatened to turn into a tsunami, and he didn't want to hurt anybody, especially her, by saying anything she wasn't ready to hear.

"You shouldn't leave," Anna said, as if the words were torn from her throat. "I'll go. Charlotte, it was nice to meet you. How much do I owe you?"

No.

Jacob wouldn't be able to live with himself if Anna was the one who left the bakery, who was forced out of what seemed to be her introduction to Charlotte. So he met Anna's eyes. Shoved his hands in his pockets. "I'll be fine. You stay, please?"

She held his stare, and this time he held his breath.

Please.

She swallowed. Seconds turned into minutes.

Finally, after he'd lost all hope she'd agree to his request, she nodded. "Okay."

The deep, gusty sigh of relief wasn't something he wanted to hide. He didn't even try. "I'll see you later, Charlotte." He left, still covered in a combination of flour and sugar, too completely messed up to care.

≫≫✴≪≪

ANNA COULDN'T HELP but watch as Jacob left the shop, whether it was solely because she wanted to make sure he'd gone or because he still fascinated her after all of those years. He was a hard habit to break despite the evidence she should.

"What was that?"

Forgetting she wasn't alone was a horrible idea. Especially in a place where she was trying to fit in, much less figure out. All she could do was shrug.

"You know," Charlotte continued, "as long as I've known him, I have never seen that."

"I'm not sure what you mean."

"Full disclosure: Jacob's one of my husband's closest friends and spends a ton of time at my house watching rugby and beating my husband at poker."

"So you're…I'm not following."

"Well." Charlotte paused, and Anna wondered what judgment was going to fall out of her mouth. "I've never ever in my life seen him rumpled, covered in flour, a mess both outside and in. And you're not much better it seems. So."

"So?"

"I figure as someone who actually lives here, it's probably my job to make sure you're protected from the nonsense."

Nonsense. Gossip.

"I don't follow. I mean, I know about gossip, and I know about how it works. Yes, I spent my summers here with my grandparents, but the rest of the year I spent in Hollowville."

"Well," Charlotte said, "this gossip train focuses on Jacob."

Jacob was at the center of Rockliffe Manor society now, like his parents had been before, like his grandparents had been before, and so on. "That I know."

"That means everybody not only wants a piece of him, they also want to claim him. He's theirs, which means people who cause him trouble, people who could obscure their path to him, and people who hurt him? The hounds go wild, and anything that person wants to do? Not happening."

Which meant if Anna's relationship with Jacob deteriorated further, as if that were even possible, life would be awful for her grandmother.

"I see," she said, the realization hitting her hard. "I…"

"Listen. I've lived here about a year or so. And I've come to the very clear conclusion that this town needs new blood and excitement. You seem like someone who's open to new things but yet is very well aware of the importance of traditions. I figured you and I were going to be friends when you told me to choose something for you, and now I'm sure you're going to need some good ones."

The truth of Charlotte's words sank in, and Anna felt herself nodding. "I will," she said. "Thank you."

"It's fine. People call me Hurricane Charlotte. Well"—she paused—"the ones I like, that is. The ones I don't, well…" She shrugged. "Anyway, you're probably looking for your grandmother's challah?"

Anna reached up to scratch the back of her neck under her sweater. "She actually said she wanted one but didn't tell me from where."

"I think your grandmother likes hers better"—Charlotte pointed out the door to the tea shop—"but I've been playing with a few recipes, and I think she'll like this one." She reached into the case in front of her and pulled out the most beautiful, golden challah Anna had ever seen.

The tantalizing aroma transported her to Friday night dinner with her grandparents, and in more recent years, just her grandmother. If it tasted half as good, she'd lose her mind.

"Stunned, right?"

"Sure, from normal people, but you have a gift."

Charlotte smiled. "Thank you, but you haven't tasted it yet. It was a resolution after watching someone make a complete mess of it on a cooking competition. Braided bread is the best. No butter, just perfection and awesomeness."

"This is so, *so* good. I can't even describe it. How much do I owe you?"

"Nothing."

"That is absolutely ridiculous. You seriously have to let me give you something for it."

Charlotte shook her head. "Call it advertising because it's the first one. If Celia Green likes it, I'll be thrilled. And if she doesn't, I'll hear about it forever or at least for the next few years at the Chamber of Commerce meetings."

"Oh!" Anna took the challah. "Right. Chamber of Commerce. Is there someone on the board who deals specifically with festival infrastructure?"

"There is, yes. She is a fascinating woman, but to be fair, anybody who does anything civic in this town has to be in order to deal with Rose."

Rose. Of course. But all the same, Anna nodded. "She's still as involved as ever?"

"Yep. Adding me to the Chamber didn't mean she was going to step down. She still has so much influence here that she's not afraid to fight against things she doesn't like or back the things she does."

"Nothing's changed then, I guess."

Charlotte shook her head. "Not really."

"And thank you, by the way."

"Oh, you're welcome." Charlotte beamed, clearly realizing Anna meant the thank you for a bunch of different things. "Trust me. It is more than my pleasure. In fact, you should go see my friend Rivvy Lehman in the records department at town hall about the Chamber of Commerce. See if she can get you the information you need."

And as she headed out the door, Anna was excited about what was to come. She'd found the beginning of a social life that didn't directly involve Jacob and had managed to get past her first interaction with him unscathed.

Everything from here was going to be a piece of cake.

FRIDAY NIGHT DINNER with his mother was important, and so Jacob continued to indulge her. A long, formally set table, with silver rarely used except on nights like this. But tonight, instead of the warmth of the candles, the mood caught the chill of the formal dining room. His mother raised an eyebrow. What was going on?

"You're leaving on Wednesday."

"Yes," he replied, the challah soft like butter on his tongue. "Leaving on Wednesday, back in time for the meetings on Thursday and Friday. Red-eye."

"You know Anna is going to be in the archives starting on Tuesday, right?"

"No," he said, calmly despite how his blood was raging, the challah turning to ash in his stomach. "I know that you're meeting with someone on Monday about potentially curating an exhibit within the historical wing during Summer Days. I know that the Historical Society is involved. I did *not* know that the person you were speaking to was Anna."

"Your powers of reasoning are fading, Jacob. You're spending too much time burning that candle of yours at both ends." His mother sighed as he tried desperately to hold himself together. "You saw her, I take it?"

"I was surprised enough to see her; I didn't ask her any questions." Surprised barely covered the emotions he'd felt. But that would do for now.

"Jacob, you really need to pay more attention to this. It's important. It's your *legacy*."

His mother was up to something, and he didn't want any part of it. He also didn't like the idea of Anna being tied up in it either. "It's not my legacy," he replied. "My legacy will be the good I do. It's my family history, yes, but not my legacy. And when people tie the two together, way too often it changes them for the worst."

"Well," she replied, "what happens when people forget is never good either. We need to write *ourselves* back into the narrative. Tell our stories. Our way. So that the words they read, the history they learn, includes ours. We have hidden for too long and have permitted our desire to hide to put us in danger. What is that saying? It's better to stand up and speak than be remembered for your silence."

"But sometimes just being silent and doing the work keeps you alive. Conspiracy theories tie deeply to anti-Semitism; 'Jews with money are evil' comes out when you break every single one of those moldy conspiracy theories open, not to mention how they fly the flag of 'Jews control the media' every time someone steps up publicly." He sighed, took a glass of water. "The footnote to *every single conversation* about us ends with how we control the government. Do you realize that I have to keep my involvement in helping organizations that fight family separations and the atrocious situation at the border silent because if my name gets mentioned, the discourse surrounding my involvement will derail the work of the organizations I'm helping?"

"You know," his mother replied, "I do know that. I am *also* from the side of your family that lost a large number of members to the Holocaust. It is a real thing and not as far away from contemporary times as people might expect. And yet I am still standing up, still forcing people to take note of us." His mother paused, watching him.

"You know," she said into the space between them, "If anybody understands how important it is to remind people that Jews have lived everywhere and that our happy-ever-afters existed, it's Anna. She has the power and understanding of history to show that what we did, just by breathing together, breaking through their views of us, was a radical act."

"I trust Anna," he replied. "I still don't trust her boss, and I don't trust the fact that you took this long to tell me she was coming."

"Well considering how you're reacting, tell me how wrong I was in waiting?"

"This isn't some silly conversation, Mother. More importantly, Jemima Kellerman doesn't deserve to have her fingers anywhere near the archives, not in person and definitely not by proxy."

"Anna isn't just a proxy for Jemima, and if you don't know that, you don't know her."

"I do know her. And if you shove her into the middle of yet another power struggle, I will be…"

"You will be what?"

His mother's expectant expression banked the fire he wanted to breathe all over everything. He forced ice into his veins once again and settled down. He took a breath. "Fine," he bit out.

"That's very good. You should also know I have meetings on Tuesday and Friday, so you'll be around to supervise Anna on those days, hmm?"

"I…"

"Supervise. Be her contact in the archives. You don't have much to do on those days, right?"

He blinked. "I…"

"She'll only need basic guidance."

He shook his head. "I can't give her hands-on guidance, Mother. I can't."

"Why?"

"Because I have a lot to take care of, and my degrees are in finance, not archival history and museum curation."

His mother sighed and stood, crossing the room to sit next to him at the table. "You don't have reason to worry,

Jacob," she said, putting her arm around him. "You and she will be fine. I promise. And you'll figure this out."

Like, he supposed, he was meant to figure everything else out. Not just for himself but for most of the people he came into contact with. And fix the problems they'd created.

But who could fix his?

Chapter Four

AFTER AN UNEXPECTED afternoon call from Charlotte to see how she was doing after Jacob's snowman impression had made the local gossip mill, Anna was persuaded to join her and Rivvy for a drink at the outdoor café on Saturday night. Although it was still late Spring, they could feel the early bits of Summer trying to push through.

Music, friends, and a new town. It was...nice. People came over to the table every once in a while, and Charlotte handled them like a pro, introducing some and ignoring others.

"They all want a piece of you," Anna said.

Charlotte shook her head after a while. "No," she said as she took a sip of her wine. "They want a piece of you."

Right. The new one, the one with the history. And, of course, the story of Jacob leaving the bakery covered in flour the day before was mentioned in a few conversations.

Aaaah, small towns.

But Anna nodded all the same, smiled and clinked glasses with her new friends, even as a hush rolled over the crowd.

She raised an eyebrow as Charlotte shook her head.

"I didn't think they'd be here," she said. "Tony said they were going to be at Ciampi's, inside. Not here."

"Orchestrated friend nights?" Rivvy asked, her hazel eyes wide. Anna tried to figure out what to say.

Charlotte sighed. "I tried." She turned toward Anna. "I wanted you to relax and enjoy yourself, you know? Get to know the town."

Anna nodded. "It's fine. For whatever it's worth, I appreciate that. But it's a small town, and we know they don't work that way."

But she couldn't have mistaken the expression on Charlotte's face as the guys settled down. Pure relief. "They're on the other side of the café, so there's no chance of them coming near here. If I see those faces getting any closer, I *will* cause some serious trouble."

"It's fine," Anna repeated as if she weren't just trying to convince them but herself as well. "It's really fine."

And it was until she had to get up and grab a drink. It had been a great night, which meant by the time she needed a refill, the servers had long since clocked out for the night. Luckily, the bar serving their portion of the café was still open. She wasn't the only one, of course; there was a line out the door of people waiting to be served.

Anna held her breath and walked up to join them. She followed the line inside and found an open spot at the bar near the wood paneling at the edges. She waited, and when it was almost her turn to order, she bumped into the person standing next to her.

Instantly, she looked over to apologize…and met Jacob's eyes. She could see tight wariness in his steel-blue gaze. It hurt.

"You look so horrified to see me that if I didn't know you better, I'd be offended," she said.

"But you do know me better?"

Did she? Was it something Anna wanted to admit here and now? "You didn't think I'd be going to get a drink?"

He nodded back, and it was like coming up for air after swimming underwater for the length of the pool. She hadn't been set up for an emotional ambush.

"Charlotte would offer to buy," he said, as if he was being forced to talk. "I expected I'd run into her, you know?"

"She did. I'm impressed."

"Impressed that I have logic at my disposal or impressed that I was so wrong?"

She shrugged, tapped the bar. "Probably the latter."

"Can I buy you whatever you're trying to order?"

"Why?"

There was a long silence between them. She was used to telling him he couldn't buy her things; she just wasn't used to being wary of his motivations. An important boundary to make in this stage of their…relationship.

If he didn't take this seriously, she would get a glass of water and pour it on his head.

"Call it a peace offering," he finally said in that way of

his that made her think he'd gone over his words in his head, as if this was what had visited him when he couldn't sleep. "I know I make things difficult, and I'm sorry. I don't want things to be awkward."

She hadn't expected this explanation, especially after he'd left Charlotte's bakery covered in flour. "I think we're long past awkward now," she replied. "Parallel universe, twilight zone, all of that. But."

He raised an eyebrow. "But?"

"Peace offering. Truce. This doesn't mean we're okay."

"This means we're back to a détente."

The tension left her shoulders. "Then you can buy me a drink."

In very Jacob-like fashion, he nodded and simply got the bartender's attention. If the rest of their problems could be solved so easily, she'd be thrilled.

A TWISTED WEB he and Anna wove, then and always.

Morals and sense were important to Jacob, and he valued them both too much to break past the boundary she'd set. Even *looking* like he was invading her space for any reason was too much.

But she'd consented to his peace offering. Granted a détente, an action that once again tangled them together in ways neither of them fully understood. All he knew was that he didn't want to lose her. Her friendship, or whatever connection they'd once had, was too important to him, and he'd guard the dying embers of that connection with his life.

"What are you thinking?" she asked.

He turned to meet her eyes as he watched the bartender pull together the order. "A lot," he said. "Monday. Your meeting."

"Yeah," she finally said. "You're going to step in? Cause havoc?"

He shook his head; the idea of intervening in her career in any way shape or form made him nauseous. "Never. Ever." He did not tell her how much he wanted to leave town while that interview was happening. Instead, he settled on telling her something more important. "I think you can do whatever you set your mind to."

"Why, then? Why did the foundation always deny the museum's request?"

"The foundation is my mother, not me," he replied. "Though I will say that your boss is awful. Horrible. I don't trust her."

"And I can handle it," she replied. "I can do my job. I can handle *her.*"

He nodded. "I trust you. Completely and totally."

"Thank you," she said.

For what, he wasn't sure. She could be talking about so many things in this set of seconds gathered together. He didn't want to guess. But what he could say was simple.

"Always."

ALWAYS.

Anna took a breath and made her way out of the bar, carrying her Shirley Temple and heading back to the table. She tried not to follow Jacob with her eyes as he wove his way through the crowd. Tried not to see the relief in his shoulders as he sat down at a table on the other side of the café.

"You okay?"

Anna nodded at Rivvy; she could see concern in her friend's pale features. She wasn't, but it wasn't something she was going to dissect at the café in person.

Being here, in Rockliffe Manor, a town full of memories that included Jacob, was hard.

No.

There wasn't a word to describe the level of difficulty this was, having him close enough to touch, tied together by history and emotion all tainted in ways she could barely understand. Especially when she was sitting at the place where they studied for college tests, outside where his smile lit up the sky as he shared the notes he'd gotten at the uber expensive test prep course he was taking.

Instead, she took a swallow of the Shirley Temple, the first drink she'd had with him. He'd gone right up to the bar, as sure now as he'd been at fifteen, and ordered, his voice level and comfortable.

But that trip down memory lane was unproductive. She yanked herself back to reality and smiled at Charlotte's dubious expression. "I'm fine," she said. "I'm really fine. So tell me what summer in Rockliffe Manor is like *now*?"

Charlotte raised an eyebrow but set the scene, letting Anna fall into the detailed description, shoving the past further and further behind her.

⟫⟫⟫⟪⟪⟪

THE PHONE BLARED in Jacob's ear the next morning before he could think. "Hello?"

"What the hell happened last night?"

He sat up, rubbed his eyes. Charlotte. "What do you mean what happened last night?"

"I tried to get the story from Tony and no dice. So what the hell happened?"

"The café wasn't my idea," he said.

"I don't care about why you were at the café," she replied. "What I care about is that you ran into Anna at the bar."

Right.

"And what really makes me confused is that I don't know whether she was more spooked after seeing you on Friday or more spooked after she was leaving the bar last night. If you ever want to be invited into that kitchen again, my friend, you need to tell me what happened."

Friday. When he left the bakery covered in flour and sugar with barely a word of explanation, and last night where he did everything he could think of to try and get them back to solid ground.

"I'm sorry," he said. "It's a long story. And I'll tell you the whole thing when you have a chance, when you're in the mood to listen."

"Come for brunch. Tony's getting up. I have things cooking."

"I'll be there."

He took a quick shower, dressed, and headed back to his car, grabbing a bag of coffee he'd bought for Charlotte in Texas.

"Pastrami egg rolls from a recipe I couldn't get out of my head, so you're getting to taste them," was Charlotte's greeting. If she was feeding him pastrami, she couldn't be that angry.

He took one from the tray and smiled back at her. "Thank you."

"So what's the story with Anna?"

"Honestly?"

"Honestly. Don't bullshit me, Jacob."

Million-dollar question if he'd ever heard one. He could barely figure out how to explain himself and he'd gone through it twice in the car. "I don't know where to start."

"From the beginning?" Charlotte shook her head and walked into the kitchen. "Come on. I have a table that needs setting and a few more things I have to make before I drag my husband downstairs. And you *will* explain what you mean."

He followed Charlotte into the kitchen, trying to find the right words. "Anna and I have known each other in varying capacities since we were kids. We've been...tied and entangled."

Charlotte found her way back to the front of the stove and tasted what looked like a sauce. "Okay, but that still doesn't explain either the snowman routine or the appearance last night."

He sighed, got himself a mug, and poured some coffee. "The power dynamic is so skewed between us, and it's made worse because I have a tendency to let my tongue get ahead of my brain around her. And because I'm trying to stay out of the way so that she can find a touchstone in this town that has nothing to do with us or her memories of childhood or her grandmother." He blew out a breath and stared through the window.

Charlotte poured some oil in a pan and gestured toward the table. "Table's still not set, so come on. Get to work."

He pulled open a drawer and took out a handful of paper napkins. "Things are hard between us at the moment, and so she's getting settled, chatting to you at the bakery, and there I was, suddenly showing up like...I don't know. It's like I'm trying to manipulate everything behind the scenes."

"Like her own personal deus ex machina, which freaks you out and sends you into the street, covered in flour."

He nodded, put a few napkins by plates before heading back to the silverware drawer. "We talked about it yesterday, actually, while we were waiting for drinks. I hope she understands that all I want is for her to be happy. But I guess she doesn't, because why was she spooked?" He blew out a breath. "It's frustrating. I don't know the right words to say to her."

Charlotte folded her arms and stared at him. "Interesting," she said, in a way that made him nervous. "And now," she said, "it's time to eat."

Chapter Five

JACOB'S VOICE WAS still ringing in Anna's head Monday morning.

I trust you. Completely and totally.

But she had spent enough time fantasizing about his voice. More than enough time dissecting the impact of his tone and his syllables. She had a meeting in a few hours; she forced herself to turn toward the kitchen table and the documents she'd printed out from her grandmother's desktop. The exhibit plan itself was a general sketch; she hadn't been given enough information to do a full plan but she didn't want to go to this meeting empty-handed. She read through them one more time, then put them into a folder that she placed a tote bag, with her wallet and her keys.

Next step was coffee. She checked the website—Charlotte's bakery was open, and if she got ready quickly enough, she'd be able to get there in time to chat with Charlotte before the meeting. Otherwise, she'd go to the library.

Having planned out her itinerary, Anna pulled her stuff

together, kissed her grandmother goodbye, and headed into town. When she turned into the small lot behind the bakery, there was a *parking space* available, leaving her very grateful for miracles that didn't require nine candles to celebrate.

Even from here, she could tell that the focus of the early morning commerce at the center of Rockliffe Manor were the two coffee shops. Their lines wound down the sidewalk.

Secure in the knowledge she'd end up with good coffee, she opened the door to the bakery.

"Anna!"

"You're here!"

"Where would I be on a Monday morning?" her friend replied.

Anna laughed. "True. Very true. Consider that me being glad to see you."

"I'll take that," Charlotte said before she turned to look up at the clock. "How much longer do you have before the meeting?"

"I've got an hour before I need to head over to the Historical Society. I'm a bit nervous."

"So sit down," Charlotte said, with a smile and a wave of her hand. "Talk to me. Keep me company for a bit."

Relief filled Anna's bones as she took the offer like the lifeline it was. Anna didn't know how else to describe it. "Absolutely."

Charlotte reached around and poured some really good-smelling coffee from a pot into a cup and passed it over.

"Excellent. I especially want to know how you're doing after Saturday."

The all-important silver lining, except for the fact that Charlotte was a new friend and deserved to know what was going on with her. "Not much to discuss," she said. "I'm a boring person in general, you know, so it was a pretty slow Sunday. I caught up with my grandmother; we chatted a bit and had brunch. I also was too exhausted to do anything interesting."

"I absolutely get that," Charlotte replied.

But the conversation was a balm for sure, and Anna was mostly relaxed when she headed to her car an hour later and drove the short distance toward the Historical Society. And as luck would have it, there was also a parking space just behind the building. The less she attempted to navigate the streets at the center of town in heels, the better for her feet and her shoes.

She got out of the car and adjusted her cardigan, stopping for a second to look at the stone and brick structure. It was the same place she'd spent hours as a teenager, working, studying, and learning under Dr. Humphries. And it was that woman's warm brown-skinned face, slightly altered with time, dark hair sprinkled with gray, that met her.

"Anna Cohen! Come, come, come, I am so very glad to see you this morning."

"I'm glad to see you too, Dr. Humphries." But she was nervous, impatient.

"I have tea, as well as scones and some rugelach for you."

The tea brewed at the Historical Society was special, and she could smell it from where she stood. No wonder Charlotte wanted the recipe.

She could also smell the cinnamon in the rugelach, and if she had to guess, that it came from Charlotte's bakery.

Thinking of baked goods and conversation, Anna followed Dr. Humphries into the central room of the Society, and it wasn't just the scent of the rugelach or the tea that flew up her nose. It was also the smell of the books and papers and antique maps that filled the shelves, closets, and all of the other storage places.

The contents of the building were special, reaching back to the founding of Rockliffe Manor. Roots of paperwork detailed special codes, stories of friends and neighbors who prepared safe passage for some and a safe landing for others. And secrets that went to the grave.

"The words these walls have stored," Anna said, smiling.

It was home.

Which was both a comforting and scary thought.

"We've made a few changes," Dr. Humphries interjected, "and we've gotten some new items in the collection."

"New items?" She raised an eyebrow.

The older woman nodded. "Yes. A few estate sales, a few donations, and a few loans from a museum in Manhattan."

Her eyes perked up. "Really?"

"Yes. Some books and a few pieces of furniture. Rose

isn't here yet, so you'll have a chance to take a peek."

Rose. Jacob's mother. The woman whose fingers worked behind the scenes of most things in Rockliffe Manor. Anna would do well to remember that.

"I will absolutely do that," she said once she realized Dr. Humphries was waiting for an answer. "Thank you, by the way."

"Of course. I am just so proud of you. You're doing amazing things at the MMJH. I can't wait to see what you do when you curate an exhibit or two of your own."

"You know," Anna said, "I wouldn't be doing what I do right now if it weren't for you. You taught me the most important thing about working with history. Our role as curators is important. Sometimes to watch and sometimes—"

"To remember. To make sure nobody forgets."

"To bear witness."

The smile altered the planes of Dr. Humphries's face. "We always must bear witness."

"And," another voice said, "to help guide contemporary events by reminding people of dangerous paths the world has taken and make sure they aren't retrodden."

The cultured tones danced like a practiced ballerina. "Mrs.—"

"Rose," the older woman said. "You call me Rose, Anna. We have too much history and water under the bridge between us for any other name."

Water under the bridge was a very delicate way of putting years of forcing Anna to figure out, based on Rose's behavior, whether the older woman was playing matchmaker or barrier, whether she was friend or foe. But the ingrained manners both her grandmother and mother had taught her, as well as years of dealing with donors, employers, and Rose herself had given Anna the ability to create the appropriate mask. And having masked her expression, she nodded as she headed to the table. "Rose, then."

As the women settled down at the table, the tea was poured.

"These are exquisite," Rose said, smiling as she bit into a rugelach. "Oh, this is a great start to our conversation."

"Yes," Dr. Humphries said. "I'm looking forward to hearing what you propose."

"Yes," Rose said as she put her teacup in the middle of the saucer. "So what did you have in mind, Anna?"

This was what she had come prepared for. Specific, distinct questions about the potential progress of the exhibit and how she intended to use the archives. She reached into her tote bag and pulled out the exhibit plan she'd put together. "I'm not sure what you have available or the kind of information you want to make accessible, but I was thinking about finding information about the first of the family and their story."

Rose used her smiles like flowers, or fans, delivering coded messages in the turn of her lips. This one was a receptive smile, but not the one Anna was looking for.

"While I think the idea of knowing more about the ancestral founding of Rockliffe Manor and the building of Rockliffe itself is wonderful, I'm not sure this is the kind of story we want to tell for Summer Days."

Anna reached for her pen and prepared to take notes. "What did you have in mind?"

"What I think is, you should think about this year's theme, which is community building. And you should think about that theme in conjunction with a way that highlights Jewish people falling in love, being happy. Because we have. In good times, in bad times, we fall in love. We are still here, and as so many others have said—"

"We are our ancestors' happy endings."

Rose bestowed the smile Anna had been looking for. Her eyes were bright, and there was excitement in her face. "That is the tie-in exhibit I want in the house as we open for Summer Days."

Anna nodded. "I can see that. Love and community building, defying the odds as we create something special. Being in love and happy."

"Yes. It's important, because it's necessary to remember that depicting Jewish people falling in love on the page or on screen or in history books can be a radical act," Rose added. "People often want us to fall into a particular, secondary, stereotypical role. Telling stories of our own, and creating narratives that place us in starring roles is a way to combat that. To ensure that we, and our history, are not erased."

The ideas were already flowing, pending, of course, on what they had in the archives and the Jewish Center's theme. "I can absolutely do this," Anna said.

"I knew you would," Dr. Humphries said. "I knew you'd be able to run with the inspiration."

Rose nodded. "Yes. I have absolute faith in Anna. Do you have any questions for me?"

"Actually, have either of you seen specifics about what the Jewish Center is doing for their booth?"

"I can answer that, Anna," Rose interjected, "because I'm on the committee. As a side note, you should also suggest that your grandmother join me there."

Anna smiled. "She's told me you've asked, but I haven't gotten a definitive answer. I think it's a good idea, for what it's worth."

"Good. Yes. I'll talk to her at our next painting night. From what I've heard, I think the Jewish Center research circle is heading towards an exhibit which is actually going to go back to the founding of the Jewish Center and the first steps toward building a Jewish community here."

"That sounds fascinating." Anna tried not to beam as brightly as she could. "So many things to think about. Should we somehow tie the exhibit in the wing with the Jewish Center's exhibit?"

"I don't think there needs to be a direct tie, but if you can find some mention of some of the founding couples in the Jewish Center, that might be a nice nod."

"Oh that kind of information would be wonderful to add in. And photographs too."

"I can see the excitement in your eyes," Dr. Humphries said. "Any other questions you might have? Is there a reason you mentioned the festival committee?"

Anna nodded. She was back on track. "Yes. I want to know who to talk to about the website because I have a recommendation, actually. A friend of mine from Hollowville, Batya Averman. She was responsible for the revamp of the Hollowville Hanukkah Festival website."

"She did an outstanding job," Dr. Humphries said. "I'd love to see if she'd be willing to do a site for the Historical Society."

Without further pause, Anna wrote down Batya's phone number and email address on two slips of paper. "Here," she said as she gave them to the two older women. "Tell her I've sent you."

"Excellent." Rose made a few notes on her own phone. "We have made a great deal of progress today, more than I intended to, actually, so we are in a very good position. Come by the house tomorrow morning, Anna, and either Jacob or I will take you to the archives."

"That sounds great," Anna said, already thrilled at the idea of discovering what stories those archives would tell her. Not to mention, learning those stories would bring her much closer to getting the exhibit of her dreams.

Even if she had to deal with Jacob to do it.

JACOB FOUND HIS way to the study the next morning and discovered, unsurprisingly, that his inbox was full. Tons of proposals forwarded from Tony or contracts from Ken, his attorney and the third member of the local branch of the Mitzvah Alliance, emails from three rounds of grant recipients wanting his help and advice. Not to mention questions from Tony about a few investment proposals and preparations for funding the new grant.

All of which screamed for his attention.

If that weren't enough, he needed to make headway on the list his father had left him with. The Mitzvah Alliance partnership papers were signed, which meant the penultimate task was done, the one that had entwined most with his own goals.

Now, only one task was left, one final wrong his father wanted him to make right. And as intensive as each task was, solving the problems his father had created was important. Because how could he make the world better if he didn't fix the problems in his own house?

Despite all of that, there was something just under his skin that wouldn't calm, more and more as Anna's voice rang through his head.

"You're going to step in? Cause havoc?"

That's what Anna thought of him. No wonder she didn't want to see him. But that was why he'd told her, in the dim light of the bar on Saturday night, that what boiled his blood was the fact that her career would be forever tainted by her association with Jemima.

Cause havoc?

Never. Ethics were important, and despite everything else said and portrayed about men of his particular ilk, he had them. There were problems he could solve, things he could do, like answer the multiple emails and solve other small emergencies that were most likely waiting for him.

Going over that scenario again in his head wasn't the best use of his time.

So he took a drink of water from the bottle he'd left in his office, rolled up his sleeves and started reading. Somehow he went from task to task, emailing notes to his virtual assistant and answering some of her questions until his phone buzzed against the desk. He picked it up to see a text from Tony.

Lunch at Ciampi's.

He needed a breather.

Already.

The decision was an easy one, and of course it had nothing to do with the fact that the restaurant was at the center of town. Not far from the Historical Society. At least that's what he continued telling himself as he stood, put his desktop computer to sleep, left the house, and headed toward the Italian restaurant.

But ordering a late lunch didn't clear Jacob's head, nor

did sitting with his friends waiting for their orders of fried ravioli and deep-dish pizza.

"Earth to Jacob," Ken interjected. "Earth to Jacob."

He blinked, following his attorney's pale hand as it blurred in front of his eyes, and yanked himself back to the restaurant. "Sorry. I'm a bit distracted."

Tony barked out a laugh. "Of course you're distracted. Considering…" He pointed toward the front door of the restaurant.

Following the direction his friend was pointing, he saw Dr. Humphries from the Historical Society with…Anna.

He couldn't help but search for telltale signs in Anna's face. Joy. Happiness. He took a deep breath. The meeting had gone well.

Except on closer inspection, it was obvious she hadn't moved from the doorframe.

Was she going to leave because he was here? He couldn't let that happen. "Be right back," he said as he dropped his napkin.

He crossed the restaurant, greeting Dr. Humphries before stopping in front of Anna. "It's good to see you," he said. "You're welcome to join us"—he pointed toward the table Ken and Tony were sitting at—"but it looks like you and Dr. Humphries have your own business to take care of."

"We do," Anna said. "But thank you."

"No problem." He smiled, relieved by her response. "I really just wanted to say hi and keep things from being awkward."

"So you don't have to leave covered in tomato sauce and Parmesan?"

He laughed. "No," he replied. "I don't think anybody would let me hear the end of it. But I just wanted to say hi, and that…"

"It's okay?"

Jacob nodded. "It's okay."

Her sigh of relief hit him all the way through to his toes, and if nothing else, this would make the rest of the summer easier for the both of them.

Chapter Six

ANNA ARRIVED AT Rockliffe the next morning to see Rose standing in front of a table filled with pastries and coffee and all sorts of breakfast food.

"I probably ordered enough to feed an army, but I wasn't sure what you'd like."

"Coffee. I ate at Oma's before I came." She smiled apologetically.

"Great. I'll just leave out some things that won't need to be chilled. As you pour your coffee, I'll give an introduction."

She nodded and moved toward the coffeemaker. Sweetener, milk, perfection.

"We have a partially organized and fully accounted for collection," Rose began. "There are things we have records of, but we don't have records for everything."

Anna smiled, braced herself. This was going to be interesting. "What happened? Why?"

"Somehow, the archivist hired by one of my relatives lost interest," Rose said, her tone a clear indication of the distaste she felt for the person who dropped the project midway.

"We still aren't sure who it was. Either way, we have more documents than records. If you would like to record the unrecorded documents as you encounter them, you are welcome to, and we can discuss that further at some point."

Maybe doing a little cataloging might get Rose to agree to give some of the collection to the museum, at least for the purposes of Jemima's exhibit. Not to mention, Anna found herself wondering what the uncatalogued items looked like.

"How about you show me to the archives now, and I'll come back later to pore over the records before diving in."

Rose smiled. "That sounds lovely."

The archives were in a building that used to house the stables, and as they opened the door Anna tried to keep her jaw from hitting the floor.

"The building is temperature controlled," Rose began, by way of introduction. "And the floors are variably temperate, which is lovely during the winter."

"I… This is impressive," Anna managed, trying to keep her voice level and professional.

"It's a crowning achievement," Rose replied, smiling. "Are you ready to get started?" she asked.

Anna nodded. "I am," she replied, not wanting to question her luck.

Taking her cue, Rose went through a basic explanation of the archives, including the rules of researching and the fact she wanted gloves to be worn when touching photographs.

Which meant there weren't just documents but photographs as well.

Wow.

There was so much here and Anna couldn't wait to get started.

A tap against the floor made Anna look up into Rose's eyes. "Aaaah," Rose said with a smile. "There you are. Do you have any questions?"

Questions were the bare minimum of things she had. Exclamations were first, pushing aside memories of years of studying in various cramped locations, hoping and wishing for a sign of historical proof. And now she was in a wonderland, decorated with shelves and shelves of boxes.

"This is amazing," she managed, even though she knew she sounded like the kid in the historical candy store she probably was. Who knew how many of the items in the boxes were unaccounted for, what stories hadn't been told?

Of course, she realized that Rose was standing there, probably expecting some kind of answer or response or something. "I...wow. I'm honored, really."

"You're a true student of history," Rose replied, smiling. A real smile. Which was good. "You know," she continued, "my mother-in-law continued the collection process, but I think she also began the process of converting this building into what you see. She saw it as her responsibility, not necessarily something that was important to her. But this? This is important, and I know you understand why."

Anna nodded. "Not because of the name but because of

the events."

Rose beamed. "This is why I wanted you to work on this project. This understanding of the importance of the role people played in world events and how vital it is to not erase perspectives."

Anna tried her best to put her professional mask in place, desperately searching for memories of what her boss had looked like when glad-handing donors. "Well, that's wonderful, Rose. Thank you ever so…"

"Let's not let a false sense of unknowing cramp our style, hmm?"

Anna blinked, clutching her tote closer to her. "I'm sorry?"

"We talked about this on the phone, dear," Rose continued as she led the way. "We have a great deal of history between us. And now, as I said then, I expect you to treat me as if I am someone you have history with."

The more Rose spoke, the more Anna lost control of not only the situation but also her place in it. She wanted Anna to treat her with…familiarity? "I'm so confused," she admitted.

"I am always confused," Rose said. "It doesn't get easier as you get older, it simply adds more decisions onto the framework."

And for some reason, those words made it somewhat easier. Anna was a professional. She had a job to do, and she'd sort out her emotions later. But to Rose, she said, "Let's continue."

JACOB HAD GOTTEN up at the crack of dawn and left the house, in favor of getting work done at the foundation offices in the center of the business district. He had so much to take care of, what with both establishing the local arm of the Mitzvah Alliance and preparing for the next round of grant applications. That and, of course, he didn't want to interfere with Anna's work.

"We need to remember," his grandmother had said when other members of his family asked her what she was doing. "We need to take stock of what we have been, what we've done. Who we are."

He'd ended up outside the archives during the walk he'd taken the night before, marveling at what his ancestors had done with an old stable building, bright industrial lights against a night sky. But he couldn't get himself to go inside. He hadn't even managed it when he'd had trouble sleeping. Because it wasn't just a building, wasn't just a warehouse.

It was history.

Visions of what Anna would do in that warehouse made him giddy. And so at the end of the day, he stopped off at Goldberg's, got a few deli sandwiches, and brought them to Rockliffe with a few cans of the soda they'd drunk during the summers of their childhood. He figured if she wasn't there, he'd leave the leftovers in the refrigerator for another night.

But because he'd known her forever, he wasn't surprised to see her grandmother's car in the drive closest to the archives.

He picked up the bag and held his breath as he walked the gravel pathway. Gave a slight knock on the door.

"Anna?"

"Oh!"

There was a shuffle of footsteps as the door opened.

His heart stopped. Skipped a beat.

Her hair was all over the place, her eyes wide, as if she'd been focused. "Is everything okay?"

He nodded. "I didn't mean to bother you. I just wanted to make sure you were okay."

"I'm fine. I think."

He raised an eyebrow. When they were cramming for the college tests, she'd get that look in her eyes after she'd been studying for too long. The very same look she was giving him now, half exhausted, half full of enthusiasm.

Then, if she'd continued to pore over her notes, she'd fall asleep where she sat within minutes.

But now, he didn't have a blanket to put over her or a sweatshirt to put under her head. All he could do to make her comfortable was ask a simple question. "Have you eaten?"

He could tell from her expression that she was about to say she had, but her stomach growled.

"I guess not."

He smiled. "I come bearing sandwiches."

"Is that Goldberg's?"

They hadn't changed the bag, just a simple g in bright blue lettering on the brown bag, but the signature smell that heralded the arrival of something from the restaurant would never change, at least he hoped. But the fact she recognized it – the bag or the smell – anyway made him smile. And he nodded. "I even brought—"

"Black cherry?"

He nodded. "I did."

He offered her the bag, and she took out the one marked with her soda choice. "Thank you," she said. "I appreciate this."

He nodded. "I figured you'd need it, you know. I saw the car."

"I didn't realize how late it had gotten," she admitted. "I'm sorry."

"Why are you sorry? What exactly do you have to be sorry about?"

"I…"

What couldn't she say? What did she think he was doing there? Checking up on her? Supervising her?

Judging her?

"Look," he said. "I saw you here. When I stopped to pick up a sandwich on the way home, I picked up one for you too. No obligation, no nothing, no admonishing except my usual take care of yourself, and that's it."

My usual take care of yourself.

Which was probably the last thing he should have said. Usual didn't apply to them right now. They were everything but usual. "Uh, you know…I just…"

But when he looked at her, he couldn't see the fire in her cheeks and the narrow eyes that meant anger. "Détente. I get it. I'm still not ready to talk about December," she said, "but I get it."

And as he passed over the bag with the sandwich and the soda, he smiled at her. "Enjoy the sandwich. Have a good night."

"So I'll see you?"

"I'm heading out to Texas in the morning," he replied, "but I'll see you when I get back."

"Okay," she said. "Thank you. Good night."

"Good night." And as he headed back to the house to eat his sandwich, he smiled. For some reason, it felt as if some small piece of what he'd broken back in December had begun to heal. And it felt good.

Chapter Seven

*N*O *OBLIGATION, NO nothing, no admonishing except my*
usual take care of yourself, and that's it.

As Anna continued to work through the archives, Jacob's
words and his uncertain expression stuck in her head. When
they used to study for their b'nei mitzvot—he for his Bar
Mitzvah in October and she for her Bat Mitzvah in September—Jacob would bring her lunch "just because," his way of
reminding her to take care of herself.

Thankfully he was away, in Texas not on Long Island,
because she didn't know what to do with him.

She didn't know what to do for the exhibit either.

The archives themselves were a wonderland of documents and photographs and unorganized history in physical
form. She could spend uninterrupted days, if not years, in
the middle of the temperature-controlled building.

But she had a job to do: create an exhibit for the wing
that would open in conjunction with the Summer Days
festival. A festival she didn't quite understand. And that
needed to be fixed.

Which meant, instead of going to Rockliffe this morning, she headed into town, and of course, her first stop was the Historical Society, where Dr. Humphries greeted her with a smile. "How are the archives?"

"They're exciting," Anna replied. "I'm really enjoying the research. But I'm having trouble figuring out my angle."

"I understand completely. Historical exploration can be joyful and exhilarating but aimless when you don't know what story you're going to tell."

Anna nodded. "Because the family has let so few people in to research, there's really no place that's fully explored or planned out. Which means I need to create the framework for the story."

"Oh, that's lovely. Let me know if I can get you anything."

"Tea would be lovely. And also?" She blew out a breath. "I know the basic explanation as to why Summer Days exists, but there has to be more behind it than just a need for tourists to know the town's history. Is there something else?"

"Well," Dr. Humphries said, "Rockliffe Manor was founded as a sanctuary for those who needed it, for any reason, built by a family who knew what it felt like to feel the force of the law on their backs. What you may not know is that the day after the town was incorporated, a bunch of weddings happened as the brand new houses of worship opened their doors. In the days after the founding, there were joyous ceremonies—celebrations of the beginning of a community, as well as weddings and other ceremonies that people either had not been able to have or were waiting to have."

"So, the Summer Days festival is basically a Founders Day, hidden among celebrations of community building?"

Dr. Humphries smiled. "Exactly. The town founders would never want a founders day celebration because they'd want the focus solely on the town and not on themselves; they named the town after the house for a reason after all. But it isn't lost on anybody that the Summer Days celebration ties into the history of the founding of Rockliffe Manor."

"Do you have information on the first few festivals?"

Dr. Humphries tapped her fingers on the desk. "I have information that people used to find the history of the town, but my guess is that Rivvy at the Records Office has more about the specific history of the festival."

Anna reached for a pen, took a few notes and grinned. Her day, she decided, was looking up.

⫸⫸⫷⫷

THE PHONE BUZZED as Jacob left the Tikkun Online offices in Austin after a successful meeting. Seeing his mother's number, he sighed and took out his phone.

"Hello."

"When are you getting back?"

"Tomorrow, why? Are you okay?"

"Fine but disappointed."

He sighed. He'd been spending more time in Rockliffe Manor for the last few years, this month especially. It had started when his father died, but he'd been fighting the urge to stay away because of Anna and all of the confusing feelings she brought up inside him.

"I'm not sure why you're disappointed. I've been doing this for the past—"

"Yes. That's why I'm disappointed. I told you that I'd be busy and needed you to be available for Anna."

Available for Anna. Not the archives, not her, not the house, not family business.

But Anna.

Which was strange, considering his mother had spent the past number of years deliberately separating them. "I've just finished a meeting with the Mitzvah Alliance's top choice to develop policy programs for organizations that want them. He's on board. Next I have to come back and start a new round of funding for the grant and then begin the process of seeing whether JIDS wants a policy arm."

"You're all over the place, Jacob. You need to rest, take care of yourself."

"I can't stop," he replied. "The people who are working against those people I'm trying to help won't stop, so I can't either."

"They're not going to be helped at all if you work yourself into an early grave."

He sighed as he headed to the car that would take him to the office he'd opened. "You're really not telling me this right now."

There were acquisition orders to sign, checks to okay, invoices to pay. Social justice work needed funds, needed behind-the-scenes people. He couldn't be on the front lines, so he'd make sure those people who were never wanted for anything.

He checked his emails and forwarded a list of therapists to the rest of the Mitzvah Alliance members. Each and every person on that list had been vetted by staff at a bunch of the organizations the Mitzvah Alliance served, and setting up a payment system would allow those doing the work to have access to therapists who understood, all without worrying about paying for it.

He got an email back almost instantly.

"Jacob," his mother repeated. "If I don't tell you this now, you'll be run down, exhausted, and I will have lost both my husband and my son for purely preventable reasons."

He sighed deeply. There were certain things about his father's death that fell into the non-preventable category, but discussing that with his mother was not within his mental capacity.

"So you'll be back in Rockliffe?"

"Tomorrow," he replied, making a mental note to change his flight time to a red-eye if the business he was there to take care of wrapped up.

"Good. That sounds good."

"Good enough to—"

"Know the conversation is being ended prematurely," his mother replied. "I recognize that tone in your voice. I will see you tomorrow."

He looked at the list of things he needed to take care of before he could leave. Hopefully, he'd be able to finish the list and make the flight.

INSTEAD OF ASKING her to meet at the Records Office, Rivvy suggested they meet at the Jewish Center. And considering she needed to take a look around the place, Anna agreed.

When she arrived, she couldn't stop staring. There was something wildly different about the building, and it wasn't the location, slightly outside the center of the town. It was as if the building was designed for another location, another place, but Anna couldn't tell what or where. What she did say was "This is gorgeous."

Rivvy nodded. "Isn't it? It's not like any synagogue I've ever been in before."

"This place has to have a story," she managed.

"It does. Apparently, the establishment of the Rockliffe Manor Jewish Center was, in fact, the reason for Rockliffe Manor's incorporation."

"You're kidding me."

Rivvy shook her head. "Nope. According to the records I've seen, Rockliffe was located in another town beforehand. The local government objected to having a synagogue in town, so the Horowitz-Margareten family literally yanked a room from their house, dropped it just beyond the borders of their property, and turned it into a synagogue for the small Jewish community. Then they moved to incorporate Rockliffe Manor as a separate town."

The more Anna learned about the town and the family, this slice of history—both past and present—the more fascinated she became. "That's what Dr. Humphries meant when she was talking about community building. The Jewish community here was celebrating the founding of the synagogue."

"Yep. The rest of the communities were celebrating the life-cycle events they couldn't because there wasn't accessible clergy." Rivvy smiled. "The chutzpah of this family. But yes. That's really why Rockliffe Manor is the way it is, and why the Jewish Center looks like it does."

"I wonder if there are records of the original building?"

Rivvy laughed. "I don't know. That would be interesting though. Unfortunately, because of the circumstances, a bunch of the records got lost between the incorporation and the synagogue placement." She paused for a second. "I think the building commissioner might be looking into it, because they're debating a motion to make the Jewish Center a historic landmark."

Of course now that she knew the story behind it, she appreciated the Jewish Center's beauty even more. The style of the building was completely incongruous with the architectural styles of the town, but fit with Rockliffe's sweeping lines and curves. Which was something Anna absolutely wrote down as she walked into the building. "I didn't know."

Rivvy shrugged. "It's a part of the history of this town. The Baptist Church also got help from the Horowitz-Margareten family, but I'm not sure about the other buildings. That," she said with a smile, "would take research."

"Fair," Anna replied as she followed Rivvy down the hall and through the building, stopping just outside a door that was labeled Library.

But it wasn't a quiet night; as they stood in the hallway, Anna could hear voices engaged in what sounded like spirited debate. "So what's going on here tonight?"

"We have a research circle, and so we're thinking about what we want the Summer Days booth to be like."

Anna nodded as they pushed open the door, and stepped over the threshold onto the carpeted floor.

Bookshelves surrounded them, filled with volumes large and small. And a group of people of all ages, each of them on chairs and couches, suddenly stopped their discussion and looked up.

"Hello, everybody," Rivvy said into the silence, "this is Anna Cohen. She's a curator from the Manhattan Museum of Jewish History, on special assignment through the Historical Society doing work in the Horowitz-Margareten family archives for the festival and the opening of a wing in their house."

There were oohs and ahs, and for the first time, Anna wasn't sure whether her professional or personal credentials were under scrutiny.

"The Manhattan Museum of Jewish History, huh?"

"That's the one. I'm working under Jemima Kellerman at the moment," Anna replied, "and my current assignment dovetails quite well with the museum's Gilded Age exhibit happening in July."

Which started a fun conversation on the Gilded Age Jewish families.

"Rabbi Davidson!"

She didn't know who'd said it, but Anna found herself looking up to see the person who'd entered the room. A tall woman with closely shorn, dark, curly hair that peeked out from under her kippah. She smiled, her topaz eyes brightening the warm dark brown tones of her skin, and the front of the room. "It's lovely to meet you. Thank you for joining our research circle."

Anna grinned. "Anything I can do to encourage people who have any kind of interest in researching Jewish history," she said. "It's important for us to know our history."

"So much of us don't," an older woman with a blue tint to her hair said.

Anna smiled. "History is a lens, a way to see the world. But from the Jewish perspective, history is the foundation of Tikkun Olam. If we don't know what happened before, how can we make the world better? How can we actively work for change when we don't know the shoulders on which we stand?"

The rabbi smiled. "I like that. Very much."

"So what are all of you doing? Do you have some specific topics you're working on?"

"One group is researching the first life-cycle events held at the synagogue, and the other is researching the first synagogue board."

"I wasn't in on the initial discussions," Rabbi Davidson replied as she sat down in an open seat. "But I think it's a good decision. This brings it back to what Summer Days is supposed to be about: the communities that founded Rockliffe Manor."

And the people.

Anna would find as many photos as she could of the Horowitz-Margareten family who lived in the house as they helped build up the community they'd helped to found. And that would be the focus of the exhibit. Of celebrations and of plans held in that wing when it was truly part of Rockliffe.

"I love this," the Rabbi said after Anna explained the foundations of her idea. "And the exhibits could be tied together in a way that works for Summer Days but yet could keep the exhibit for the wing rooted to both the family and the congregation."

And as if it was nothing, the weight lifted off of Anna's shoulders. She had a plan, a framework. More importantly, she couldn't wait to get started.

⟫⟫⟫✳⟪⟪⟪

ONCE AGAIN, JACOB was exhausted and had landed in Rockliffe Manor. But this time, he was hungry. And so after the car dropped him off, he left his bags in the house and headed to Goldberg's.

As he stepped through the doorway of the restaurant, the smell wrapped around him. Corned beef, mustard, matzah ball soup, knishes, and potato kugel. They were the smells of home, of a history so much bigger than he was or hoped to be.

He looked up at the front counter and saw Anna.

"You're not leaving," she said as he met her eyes.

He smiled. "I guess I'm not."

She gestured to her matzah ball soup. "And I'm not either. This is too good for me to leave, and not to mention I have knishes coming for my second course."

"I can smell them already," he replied before he ran out of words. He didn't know how to continue the conversation, how to make this comfortable. "I'll go…to…"

Anna shook her head. "You finding a table is both ridiculous and unfair to the person who has to sweep the floor, unless you're telling me you're going to sweep the back."

And before he started to say he'd do just that, she raised a hand. "Nope. Wrong person to say that to, because you totally would. Look. Our past is radioactive, but I'm working at Rockliffe, in the wing. We should figure out how to deal with each other."

"Not just détente?"

"No. More than détente. More like…"

He could see the thought process, the gears spinning behind her eyes. Friends? Acquaintances?

"Who we'd be without our history," she said finally.

But what did that mean, exactly? A fresh start? A clean slate? But instead of asking, he said something more important. "I'll follow your lead."

"What brings you here tonight? I thought you were in Texas."

"I was," he replied. "Got in not long ago, and I'm hungry. You?"

"Long day learning about what Summer Days is." She gestured to the notebook not far from her right hand. "Making a list of what I'm looking for tomorrow in the archives."

He held the menu tightly, holding back the impulse to speak words he wouldn't let himself say he had no business seeing her list. "Cool," he said instead.

She looked at him, and he saw the way she grabbed her spoon, tightly, as if she didn't want to let it go. "Yeah. I'm excited." She paused. "What were you doing in Texas anyway?"

He smiled and told her about the office he'd set up down there, about the things that office was doing, and about the work he'd been able to finish that morning. "And so I finished the meeting and came back."

"I didn't realize," she said.

"It's fine," he said. "Everything I do works much better when people don't notice what I'm doing behind the scenes."

"I understand," she said. She took a drink of her soda as his sandwich arrived.

He picked up the mustard container in front of him, shook it, then flipped the cap before squirting it on his sandwich and replacing the bread on top instead of holding it out to offer her the pickle like he used to. "Yeah." He paused as he picked up the first half of his sandwich. "So what did you find so inspiring about Summer Days, if you don't mind my asking?"

And as she told him about the conversations she'd had with Rabbi Davidson, Dr. Humphries, and Rivvy, he found himself fascinated. The information, the tone of her voice, the scene she set.

"That look on your face," she said, her voice enveloping him just a little. "I…"

He smiled, realizing what she might have thought of. Moments where over the many years of summers, sitting on the lawn at Rockliffe, he'd been able to listen as she told him her favorite stories from school. About the things she'd learned at the Historical Society. Even when they were studying for college tests. "The way you tell stories has always fascinated me," he said. Honesty was always on the table. "No matter what those stories were about."

She blushed then. "I could never tell if I was boring you," she said. "And yet I would always be surprised when, at some point, without fail, you'd make some comment that made me realize you were actually listening."

"How could I not?" he said. "I always listen. Always."

"You did."

The end of the sentence felt premature; one of the many where it felt like she was about to say something else but stopped as if she'd decided against whatever follow-up she was going to make.

Instead of pushing her, he focused on his sandwich, the taste of the bread on his tongue, the tang of the mustard and the slight spice of the pastrami, just the way he liked it.

"Idon'tknowhatyou'redoingtomorrow but if you'd like to see what I'm up to…"

It took him a second to realize she was talking to him, even longer for him to decipher what she'd said.

He nodded. "What time tomorrow? Morning?"

She smiled. "I'd like to get an early start."

"That's fine," he replied. "I've been getting up early re-cently, so early isn't a problem."

She didn't answer immediately. Was something wrong, either with her or something he'd said? Because she was looking at him as if she was trying to see through him. Was it his motivation or the fact that she hadn't expected him to join her?

"Don't you have things you need to do?"

Of course. He always did. Things came up, things that he had to deal with. Important things that if left unattended would turn into three-alarm fires.

But this? This was important in a different way. Nothing he did would matter as much as this. The rest of his agenda could wait. "No," he said. "Nothing as important as this."

He could see the disbelief in Anna's eyes, and it hurt. He deserved every bit of it, but it still hurt.

"I'll come to the front, then. Not to the archives."

"Tomorrow morning, front door. Right." He smiled.

"And if you try to pay for my food tonight, it's off."

He could handle that bargain. "Okay," he said. "Deal." But he didn't mention lunch or the snack he was already planning.

Chapter Eight

WHAT WAS IT about Jacob that made Anna's brain short circuit?

If she could find an answer to that question, she'd buy a lottery ticket for the rest of her life.

What had possessed her to ask him to help her in the archives? She'd blame the knishes and the matzah ball soup and the smell of the cherry soda and the way the bubbles danced on her tongue.

She knew what that mix of pastrami on rye tasted like, what the pickle did to his breath.

Nostalgia was a dangerous drug. His fascination with the work she was doing and the way his face lit up when she talked about it wasn't helping.

She pulled on jeans and a pair of boots, an old college T-shirt, and a hooded sweater, shoving the rest of what she needed into a tote bag before heading out of the house. She had five minutes to get to Rockliffe, and she'd need all of them if anybody in town decided to drive anywhere.

Thankfully, the roads were clear and she remembered to head to the front door. Not the front of the archives.

And when the door opened, it wasn't Rose standing in the doorway.

It was Jacob. Standing there in sweatpants and his own old college T-shirt, his eyes slightly sleepy, his hair mussed as if he'd been raking his hands through it.

"You ready?" she asked. "You look like you just crawled out of bed."

He smiled. "I figure I'll get you a cup of coffee, we'll chat about what we're looking for, and then," he gestured toward his T-shirt and sweatpants, "I'll get changed and come into the kitchen to meet you."

"Sounds good."

She followed him inside the house, then toward the kitchen, watched as he poured her a cup of coffee. He put in sweetener and a little bit of milk, smiling shyly as he did so. He never forgot, did he?

Anna took a sip, and it tasted just right, as if it had been only minutes not years since he'd made her coffee.

She tried not to watch as he made his own. Their relationship hadn't ever been easy, but there had been benefits, of understanding and of…

Well, being able to look at him unabashedly.

That and having those intense blue eyes focus on her like she was the only person in the room. Having him there to bounce ideas off of. And how he remembered the simplest things like how she liked her coffee.

She looked up at the ceiling and took another sip. The

coffee was still perfect.

"What are we looking for?" he asked, taking a drink from his own cup. She could see the tension in his knuckles as he kept himself from clinking her mug with his own as they'd always done. "What's on the agenda today?"

"So," she began, pulling the words together. "The focus of the exhibit is going to be about the family members who helped build the community in Rockliffe, so their photographs, along with photographs of the first life-cycle events the family members were involved in, will be on semipermanent display along with descriptions and photos of the pieces they contributed to the wing. That's what we're looking for."

"Photographs. Interesting." He paused, and to her perspective he was a bit uneasy.

She wondered what he was uneasy about and decided she wasn't asking. Instead, she wanted to know what was really important. "But are you sure about helping?"

He nodded almost instantly, which was a good sign. She watched as the wheels seemed to turn in his brain, as if the words were harder. "I trust you," he finally replied. "I trust your handiwork, and I trust your understanding of history. And there's no better way to show you that than to help."

"So that's why you said yes last night?"

He nodded, because that was how Jacob worked, and if she knew nothing else in this lifetime, she knew how he worked. When he believed in something or someone, he would roll up his sleeves, or whatever the equivalent was, and get to work, showing his support not just by words but by actions. "Partially," he said. "But partially I said yes because you asked. And I wanted to be here for you." He smiled in that way of his. "And after saying that, I'm going to head upstairs to change. I'll be right back."

She watched him go, finding herself unsure. What exactly was she supposed to do with him?

She had no idea.

JACOB STARED OUT the window, ignoring the vibrating phone and the unfathomable number of emails in his inbox. So many emotions over a pair of jeans and work boots.

Except this was trust. He couldn't screw this up.

His heart was pounding in his chest, his fingers running the laces through his boots. An old T-shirt and a sweatshirt.

He couldn't screw this up.

So much was riding on this. He needed to live in the moment with her and not think about her job or his. How he hated her boss was not a permitted topic of discussion.

She didn't trust him, not in the way she had before; there was a wall, ever so slim, between them now. Even though he deserved it, even though its presence was his fault, it still hurt.

The phone beeped again with a text, and two voicemails

and five emails popped up.

He sent a quick text to his assistant to prioritize everything; he'd come back to it later.

For now, he had to head downstairs, only to confront the look in Anna's eyes that meant he'd taken too long.

She was still waiting; that was a plus. But she'd put her tote bag on her shoulder. That was never a good sign.

Instead, he smiled, tried not to notice the surprise as she saw him come down the stairs. "I'm sorry," he said. "I didn't mean to take forever."

"I honestly didn't expect you to be here at all."

"It's the thing I'm most looking forward to today."

She raised an eyebrow. "I wish I could believe you."

That hit hard. What had happened in December was the straw that broke the camel's back, but that back hadn't been stable for a while. "I know. That's my fault. But your interest in history has always inspired me."

"What? Like made you more aware of how amazing you are?"

He shook his head. He wasn't ready to be sarcastic with her just yet; he didn't even think she was. She deserved honesty, an insight into what he was thinking. "History is a lens and a path. I'm not my ancestors, but I need to deserve them and need to better myself and them." And eventually, when he was ready, open that last envelope.

"Jacob?"

He realized from the tone of her voice that she'd been

trying to get his attention for a bit, and that burned. "Yeah?"

"You'd gone somewhere else. Just wanted to make sure you were still ready for this. Still in?"

"Yes," he said, "I am. You have my full and undivided attention."

They headed silently side by side, out to the back door, the one that led right onto the patio and the shortcut to the old stables.

"Thank you," she said.

He smiled. "You—" He swallowed back the reflexive response. "No thanks necessary," he said. "It's both an honor and a privilege."

She shook her head, but he could see the joy in her eyes as they arrived at the archives.

"You ready?" he asked.

"I've been ready," she replied.

He punched in the code at the door and opened it, carefully entering the building and turning on the light. He shuddered at how powerful it was. "This is…I can't describe it."

"A treasure trove of unexamined facts?"

He laughed, and it felt good to laugh with her. Alongside her. "I'd settle with impersonal, as if it contained things that never belonged to anybody, you know?"

"Well, that's just the clothing, the protection. There's so much in here, and it all deserves to be preserved because the stories are important. The people who lived those stories are important."

"History is lived, and the second you separate it from people's experiences is the second you run the risk of erasure."

"So much erasure." She smiled, and even if it felt like gallows humor, he could live in that smile for the rest of his life.

"Tell me what to do."

She raised an eyebrow he could judge only as skeptical, an emotion he was prepared for. "You sure?"

"You take the lead. You know what you're doing. I'm only your assistant."

Anna nodded and reached into the bag she'd brought with her, taking out a box of gloves. "Put a pair on and then we'll talk."

They would be going through documents that were centuries old. Touching them with fingerprints was not an option. The gloves were hard to get on, of course, but it was important he wear them. Preserving history was important. And worth his discomfort.

Then he watched as she took out a notebook, carefully flipping through pages. He recognized bits of his mother's handwriting intertwined with his own, and when Anna stopped, he saw hers.

"We're looking for documents of the earliest community building and the decisions made by the family about the Rockliffe Manor Jewish Center, as well as specific bits of family memorabilia for the relatives who lived in the house before the historical wing was closed off. Then we look at the photographs. I have a checklist"—she brandished it—"and as we find items on this list, I'll mark them off. Sound good?"

Exploring his family history with her sounded like the perfect way to spend the morning, and maybe, possibly, the afternoon.

⇢⟫⟩⟨⟨⟨⇠

WHEN THE 1:00 p.m. alarm went off, she was surprised at how much progress they'd made.

And Jacob? She turned to see how he was doing, only he looked like he'd been woken from a dream.

"Hard work?" she asked.

"Seeing tangible reminders of the town's history is awe-inspiring, despite the fact I feel like I don't have to go to the gym for a year," he replied as she took the pile of newly cataloged documents she'd placed into separate plastic dividers.

"Inspiration and perspiration sometimes do tie together," she said with a laugh.

But when she looked at him, really looked at him, she saw that expression on his face, the one that meant he was working out some problem in his head. Within an hour, he'd give suggestions on how to fix a problem he'd noticed. "What's up though?"

"I wonder if there could be a way to organize all of the cataloging on some kind of database."

Anna paused for a second and looked up at him, knowing she could take him seriously. Which meant there was only one person she could suggest, who she trusted enough for an assignment like this. "My friend Batya designs websites, and before that she was involved in a lot of historical research. If she doesn't have a system herself, she'll know someone who does. I can ask her."

"Yes. Absolutely ask her."

"I also recommended her to your mother and Dr. Humphries for the Summer Days website, but she hasn't heard anything."

She watched as he pulled out his cell phone, typed a little bit before gesturing at the screen. "I'll poke around at the council meeting and see what I can find."

"Oh that's great," she said, smiling at him. "Do you want lunch?"

"Sandwiches?"

No frills, uncomplicated. Perfect. "Yes, please," she said.

She watched as he picked up his phone again and typed, his nimble fingers moving quickly.

"I got a bunch. They'll be here in a bit. Give us time to head over to the kitchen and wash up."

She wasn't sure what else to say as they left the archives and he locked it up. "You have a busy afternoon?"

He shrugged. "Few fires to put out, few things to take

care of. Nothing that big. However…"

A light in his eyes told her he hadn't just stopped talking randomly. "What's going on in that head of yours?"

"I have an idea, a bit of a craving, if you will."

She raised an eyebrow. "What do you mean?"

"Well." He grinned. He actually grinned, and dear God she knew what he was going to ask. "How about you finish what you want to finish for the day, I'll go upstairs and put out the fires, and we go for a drive?"

She could remember summer afternoons in his car as soon as he got his license, driving the highways, the backroads of Suffolk County. If he had a convertible that summer, the top would be down, her hair flying in the breeze, and if that summer's car wasn't a convertible, he'd have the windows down anyway. They'd drive to the beach, run on the sand, and then stop off for pie.

Pie at that perfect bakery, the one by the highway. A bottle of lemonade and two pieces of pie they'd split because neither of them could decide which flavor they actually wanted.

That mischievous grin, the look in his eyes.

And pie.

She was incapable of resisting.

"Okay. You're on."

HIS HANDS WERE sweating as he left the house, the gravel crunching under his feet. The car keys were a weight in his hand.

Both Tony and Ken thought he was out of his mind, and Charlotte insisted he was certifiable.

This was a horrible idea.

But he couldn't help himself. The words had come out of his mouth, a horribly ill-conceived dream that had somehow worked its way into his brain the night before.

And yet. She'd said yes.

It was, he knew as he headed closer to the archives, entirely possible that she'd say no at the last minute. Just like she'd expected he would when she'd asked him to join her this morning.

He blew out a breath and stopped. She was standing right in front of the archives, waiting for him as if he'd forgotten, as if she thought he'd pull his invitation and leave her behind.

"So," she said, hands deep in her pockets, perhaps trying to keep herself from moving those hands of hers. "You put out the fires?"

"I did. Extinguisher and all. You find anything else interesting?"

She laughed, and the sound of that laugh almost did him in. "Everything's interesting. Not everything I found is relevant, but it's interesting."

He wanted to know what she'd found, but it felt like too

much to ask. Instead he smiled. "I'll get the car."

She nodded, and the excitement in her eyes was a gift he didn't deserve.

He continued along the path, past the archives to the garage. The one meant for the excessive number of automobiles his father had amassed during his lifetime. Jacob's two cars seemed a lot, but he drove them into the ground, as much as he drove anything anyway.

"You still have it."

Her voice rang like a bell behind him, and he knew what she was referring to. He smiled, staring at the convertible, sitting next to the sedan he drove most of the time.

"I got this one…" He tried to remember as he ran a hand through his hair. "A year ago? Two? The one I had before was unfixable." He shrugged. It felt strange to be so careless about money around her, and not remembering making purchases like this was definitely careless. And yet. "Things have been…wild."

He knew what this looked like, but she wasn't judging him for this. The expression on her face was about other things, other places. "So you recreated a car you couldn't fix?"

"As best I could," he replied. "Yeah."

"Let's do it."

"Okay," he said, grabbing the keys from his pocket and taking them out. "Let's do this."

Sitting in the passenger seat of a convertible with Jacob behind the wheel was a definite trip at a minimum.

Anna found herself grooving to the soundtrack as he tested the car's speed on the backroads. She had been so free, so young the last time she'd done this. The last time they'd done this.

And they'd chosen a perfect time to head out to the tip of the island. Jacob maneuvered the car with expert ease along the winding back roads, and there was hardly any traffic once Jacob finally jumped on Route 25A. He pulled into a space near the small shop, and she could see his hand flex before he shoved it in his pocket as he got out of the car.

She recognized that hand flex, and not just because she was doing the same thing. She'd seen pages and pages of blog posts dedicated to the emotion that kind of hand flex showed. He wanted to take her hand.

And that would be a horrible idea. Horrible.

Instead, they walked inside, his pants brushing against hers. She glanced at his face. He looked so calm and placid, but his eyes were sapphires, sparkling with joy he couldn't hold back.

That was Jacob.

"Same?"

His voice was soft, but it busted through her thoughts, bringing her back down to earth. She glanced up at the list of slices available that day and nodded. "Of course."

And so carefully and quietly, he ordered. Two slices, two large lemonades. She waited at the counter, watching the plastic glasses as they were passed over, ice melting down the sides. He swiped up the containers with the slices, the forks and napkins; she carried the drinks to the table.

She could sit like this forever, the old wooden table, the taste of apple cherry pie on her tongue. "Thank you," she said.

He looked up from his pie, his eyes intent. "For?"

"This," she replied. "I like this kind of us."

"Me, too," he said. "This us has always been my favorite."

And for some reason his words made her wistful, because the truth was, they hadn't been *this* for a long time. This was what all of her horrible decisions about him went back to. This was what she searched for and failed to find in anybody else.

Even him.

Chapter Nine

ANNA SAT AT the Rockliffe kitchen table the next morning, organizing her notes and sipping coffee that had come with a note from Jacob.

"Fuel for today. Hope you find what you need," it read.

She took a deep breath and sighed. There she was, meeting him yesterday and having one of the best days ever.

And today? A note.

She shook her head, took a sip of her coffee, and continued to work on what the exhibit might look like instead of pondering her disappointment.

As Anna started to organize her notes her phone buzzed with a text. Picking it up, she saw it was from Sarah.

S: Meet me in front of the bookstore at 2.

She blinked and immediately texted back. **You're in town?**

S: Yes. I am. I'll tell you the story later.

A few hours later, she took her friend to sit at the outdoor café.

As they caught up over glasses of lemonade and iced tea, Anna looked up into her friend's eyes. "What you're doing is lovely," Sarah said, "but there's something wrong and you need to tell me."

Anna sighed. "Jacob is Jacobing, and I don't know what to do with myself."

Sarah raised an eyebrow as she stirred her drink. "The Jacobing you remember or the Jacobing you were crying about five months ago, when you told me to go after Isaac?"

"The Jacobing I remember. He's being sweet."

Sarah nodded sagely in a way that made Anna nervous. "Let's get real here. Jacob is both the Jacob you remember and the Jacob you were crying about. Which one he'll be will depend on the moment. You have to figure out whether you can deal with both aspects of his personality."

"His biggest problem is his inability to tell someone no. What he needs, and he's always needed, is…"

"A keeper?"

Anna grinned at the sound of Charlotte's voice, as Sarah laughed. "You're Charlotte Liu," Sarah continued, as Charlotte sat down to join them.

Anna nodded. "She's been so kind to me since I got here."

"Not to mention, my husband is Jacob's best friend from college, so I have a bit of insight into whatever's going on in that head of his."

Sarah raised an eyebrow. "Were they friends in grad school?"

Anna nodded; she hadn't met Tony when she and Jacob tried to date while they were both in grad school.

"They were both in separate grad programs, but they stayed in touch," Charlotte said. "Tony went to Stanford but came back to the city. Then there was the Thanksgiving incident, and soon after, Jacob convinced him to come out here."

Anna raised an eyebrow. "Thanksgiving incident?"

Charlotte took a sip of her own drink. "Yep. In the middle of Thanksgiving about five years ago, Tony went into the other room to organize something. We went back there, only to find him asleep on the floor. He'd been pulling all-nighters, stressing about work, and it finally caught up with him. He woke up the next afternoon, and that was it."

Anna nodded. "That would do it."

Charlotte smiled. "And it did. About three years later, he came out here and we bought the house. I opened here about two years ago, started splitting my time about a year after that."

And in the space that followed, Anna gestured at her friend. "And this is Sarah Goldman, who has been my best friend since kindergarten. She's here from Hollowville for the day."

Sarah smiled. "I had a special order to drop off at the bookstore, so I figured I'd say hello."

"For which I am forever grateful. So," Anna turned to Charlotte, "what do you think Jacob needs?"

"A reason to rearrange some of his priorities for good," Charlotte said. "Not just for the five minutes you two are in your idyll."

"I can see that," Anna said.

"See here's the thing," Charlotte continued, "telling someone no, lessening his commitments isn't going to help Jacob figure out and stick to what's important. My husband can get a hold of Jacob at any time or any place. I'd wager you could too. But that's not a consolation when you're waiting for him to arrive when and where he said he would."

Anna shook her head. "It isn't. It really isn't." She blew out a breath. "That's what I need to remember. The reason we've never worked well together is because he never prioritizes us."

And as she stirred her drink, those words ran through her head. Jacob's heart would always be in the right place. It was the rest of him that would be a problem.

➤➤➤✸◄◄◄

AFTER DROPPING OFF coffee for Anna, Jacob headed to the foundation offices to deal with some last-minute paperwork on Mitzvah Alliance business. Halfway through the day, he got a call to meet Ken for pie and sign some contracts that had come in from grant recipients.

Except he couldn't concentrate. Not on anything. Not the pie, not the conversation.

All he could think of was yesterday's drive. His heart was racing, the taste of the pie he'd ordered on his tongue. Of course, part of the problem was that he'd ordered apple cherry from this pie shop today. The very same pie he'd eaten with Anna.

At least that was what he told himself.

"Stop staring out the window," Ken interjected. "You're going to give me a complex."

Jacob shook his head. "Sorry. My mind is elsewhere."

Ken laughed. "That's what they all say, my friend. Now what's going on?"

"Don't take this the wrong way, but I don't think you're the best person to talk to about this." Luckily, Ken was a close enough friend to understand the workings of his mind.

"I'm assuming this is personal, not business?"

"Yeah. It's a personal mess I'm not exactly sure how to talk about."

"Understood. It's about relationships. Right?"

"Got it in one."

"And I am absolutely not the one to talk about this with. Especially considering I can't get my head out of my butt long enough to ask Rivvy to grab a bite after work."

Jacob took a long swallow of coffee. "I wouldn't put it like that."

Ken snorted. "Of course you wouldn't. You're too nice to put it like that. Formal too. But maybe you're supposed to do the opposite of what I would."

That was an interesting idea. "So you'd be leading by example on things I should not do?"

Ken cut into his apple pie. "Pretty much. Tell people things. Use your words. Don't forget them. Don't be me."

Use your words. Tell people things.

Express your concerns and your feelings.

"That makes so much sense." But expressing feelings didn't fix his responsibilities. Or the fact that he wasn't with her, and didn't know how to be.

⊱⊱⊰⊰

AFTER DROPPING SARAH off at the train station, Anna headed up into town to get a drink, but it was too gorgeous to go back to her grandmother's, so she went back to the outdoor café.

She made her way through the tables, waving and smiling until Charlotte beckoned her over. "Anna!" she said. "Come join us!"

And of course, *us* was her and Tony…and Jacob?

"Are you sure?"

"Yes," Jacob said, his eyes finding hers. "It would be nice."

And so Anna took the chair next to Charlotte. They were catching up, a light discussion over lemonade. And suddenly they were talking about a party.

"Party?"

Charlotte blew out a breath. "I'm having a party this weekend, and you're coming, right?"

Anna blinked.

Tony smiled. "Yep. It's one of the last weekends before summer makes things go wild out here, so Charlotte has a party. You absolutely should come." He turned to the seat next to him, to Jacob. "You coming?"

"I hope to," he said.

Charlotte raised an eyebrow. "You better," she said. "Or I'll have to go to Texas to drag you back in time."

Tony laughed. "She would, too."

"So what do you say, Anna?" Charlotte asked. "Are you going to come?"

"I'd love to," Anna said. "Is there anything I can do to help?"

"Come to brunch on Saturday and we'll organize. I think Rivvy's coming too."

"I'm looking forward to it," Anna replied. And of course, she couldn't help looking at Jacob. She didn't need him to have fun at the party, but it would be interesting to see if he actually arrived.

❯❯❯❮❮❮

JACOB PACED HIS Texas office. He couldn't get Anna off his mind.

They were all over the place, but she deserved…something.

He blew out a breath and read the text again.

Missed my coffee. Hope your flight was okay.

He replied: **Flight was okay. A lot of details. How's the research going?**

He sat down and started signing checks, requisition orders, and went over his notes for the meeting he had on the docket. He was *finally* going to talk to the head of JIDS about what they'd want in a policy arm.

The sound of his phone buzzing against his desk broke into his thoughts.

It was Anna.

He couldn't just go back to work now, so he read the message. It was a detailed explanation about her research and ended with a photo showing her in the Jewish Center library, holding a book of architectural plans.

Yep. That was Anna.

Even in a text message, her enthusiasm was contagious. He wanted to live in it.

But he couldn't. Not now.

He pulled himself together and replied.

I'm glad you're going to find what you need.

The reply was quick. **Me too. I'm really enjoying the project. So, you'll be at the party on Saturday?**

That was a question. He wasn't sure he'd make it back on time.

I won't be there at the beginning but I will try to make it by the end. He blew out a breath, pulled together his words. He needed to make them count. **If I make it, can I drive you home?**

Terrified of getting a response, terrified he wouldn't, he shoved his phone in his desk drawer and closed it. He wouldn't get anything done if he spent the next few hours looking at his phone, and that wouldn't help anybody.

Not even him.

Chapter Ten

J ACOB WAS EXHAUSTED, and the traffic was horrible. Late Saturday traffic on the Island wasn't supposed to be bad. Except it was, of course.

If he could breathe fire, there would be...a problem worse than he had at the moment.

He'd barely had a chance to drop his bags off before he had to jump into his car and drive to the industrial space where Charlotte was having her party. The valet took the keys and his tip before Jacob braced himself and headed inside.

Of course, as he stepped over the threshold, all he could hear was his own footsteps, the noise of conversation and of excitement dropped to a whisper. Because nothing else like a late arrival explained a sudden hush.

He pulled himself together, not the relaxed self he expected to be, but the one that he felt he had to be during meetings and other moments where he had to shoulder the responsibility of being the center of attention.

"I'm the hostess," Charlotte said, grinning as she headed over to him. "Glad you're here."

Her voice was comforting but he was still on alert. "Me too," he said. "The traffic on the LIE was horrible."

She snorted. "When isn't it?"

He smiled. "So it's going okay?"

But before he could say anything else, Tony approached. "Heeey. You're here."

He nodded. "I am."

"Good." Tony clapped his back and nodded to Charlotte. "We need to get you a drink."

Jacob let his friend lead him toward the bar, catching him up on a few local Mitzvah Alliance issues.

"What is this?" Ken interjected as he joined the two, passing drinks to each of them.

"Can't," Jacob said at the whiff of scotch. "I need to get some kind of soda because I'm driving."

Ken and Tony both raised eyebrows. "You're driving?"

"Yeah. I'm driving."

"What he means is," Tony interjected, "he's ready to bolt at a moment's notice because he's dead on his feet."

"That too," he said. But after he'd said it, he wished he could pull his words back into his mouth.

Tony raised an eyebrow, and Ken glared at him.

"All I'll say," Tony said, "is that whatever other driving you're doing, just be aware."

He nodded, briefly, as Ken went off to chat with one of the other attorneys in town and Charlotte beckoned him over to talk to someone else.

The party was in full swing, and he was glad he'd come. People from different parts of town, Charlotte's friends from the city and other places were there. As he began to feel more comfortable, he realized he was enjoying himself even as he moved from conversation to conversation, the warmth of spending time with friends, less time spent behind the chill of the professional mask.

But he hadn't seen everybody, and his experience taught him all too well that letting his guard down was a risky proposition.

"Jacob."

Anna's voice broke through the ice that had started to fill his veins. This time he could let them thaw. "Hi," he said.

She was gorgeous.

"You made it?" Disbelief and excitement warred in her eyes.

"I would have been here earlier, but there was traffic all the way from the airport."

"You made it," she said again, as if she'd been caught in a broken record.

"I did. I'm here." And there was nowhere in the world he would rather be.

THE PARTY WAS wonderful, and dancing with Charlotte and Rivvy, drinking sweet punch as the bright lights twinkled in the large space was just perfect.

As perfect, of course, as it could be with the question hanging over her head: did she want Jacob to drive her home?

If, of course, he could make it to the party.

Which was a huge if.

But if he did…

She stopped dancing for a bit; her perfect heels were getting a bit uncomfortable. She took them off, dropping them into a corner with so many other pairs.

Did she want him to drive her home?

Of course she did. Decision made, she headed back onto the dance floor shoeless and ready to groove.

Her dress was ideal for dancing, all twirls, except after a while, she told Rivvy she needed to get a drink and headed to the bar. Thankfully, there was an open stool. She took it, gratefully if not gracefully in the slightly below-the-knee pale blue dress she was wearing. "A glass of punch," she told the bartender. "Please. Extra ice."

She took a breath as she watched the bartender put the ice in the glass, nimble fingers reaching a ladle into the brightly colored bowl, the punch flowing into the glass with a flick of his wrist.

The tip she gave him was large, and she took the glass with both hands, settling into the stool. More of that sweet, bubbly punch sat on her tongue, and she'd never been happier.

But something caught her eye, and she turned.

Jacob. Standing there as if he wasn't sure where to go, unsure of his welcome or himself. She babbled his name and he turned.

Even his words were unsure, though he melted before her; his shoulders relaxed and the distant look that haunted her nightmares became the familiar expression of recognition and…understanding?

"You made it," she said.

She hadn't expected this scenario, not in a million years. A text Sunday morning with an apology, yes, absolutely. But not a living, breathing Jacob standing in front of her in a suit jacket and a blue tie that matched her dress.

There weren't enough words in the world for her to explain what that felt like. Exhilaration, surprise—words like that weren't enough. Promise wasn't either. Change didn't fit.

All she knew was that the die had been cast and now she had to follow through.

The thump of the bass drum invaded the space where words would otherwise go, and as she listened closer, she heard the opening notes to a song she adored. "Going to dance," she said as she dropped her glass on the bar. "Wanna come?"

Driven by the warring emotions that crossed his face and the conflict she could see in Jacob's eyes, she jumped off the barstool and headed to the dance floor, the familiar rhythm of his footsteps behind her clear in her ears.

This time when she held out her hand, just on the edge of the dance floor, he took it, enveloping her fingers in the warmth and familiarity of his.

The music beat out an invitation, and as they danced, Charlotte and Rivvy joined them, Ken and Tony on their heels. Excitement propelled their motion, and soon, fueled by punch and joy, Jacob's jacket joined her shoes on the corner.

They stayed on the floor, dancing together or in a group, fast and slow as the music changed from song to song. But when the lyrics hit her ears, telling the familiar story of a group of people who didn't want to end a perfect night, Anna realized how tired she was. How comfortable she was in Jacob's arms as he leaned in close.

"Are you ready to go home?"

His voice rumbled deeply in her ears, enveloping her in a calm she hadn't felt in a long time. And even though she didn't want to leave the moment, the feeling or the party behind, the only word that came to mind was, "yes."

Chapter Eleven

J ACOB WAS EXHAUSTED and exhilarated at the very same time. Anna had taken him up on his offer. He was going to drive her home.

"I'm going to go get my jacket," he said.

"And I," Anna replied, "am going to go and sit down, get a drink. Relax a bit." She paused. "Can you do me a favor?"

"Anything."

"My shoes," she said, a smile brightening her face as she reached up with a tissue to blot her forehead. "They're blue heels. Can you bring them over?"

"Sure."

He left Anna sitting at the bar and went to gather his jacket. And as he lifted up the jacket, he saw the shoes, bright, sparkling blue. Interesting, he decided, but for the life of him he couldn't remember if the move had been deliberate. Either way he picked up the shoes and headed back to her, returning the discarded footwear as she sat on a barstool, drinking water as quickly as the bartender could give it to her.

"This is perfect," she said, gulping down more of the water. "Thanks." She grinned at him and made his heart skip multiple beats. "I think I could drink Niagara Falls." But instead of letting him reply, she took one shoe from his outstretched hand, making his fingers blaze with heat and tension, and put it on one of her bare feet.

He watched, standing silently, patiently, as she reached again, taking the other shoe and putting it on.

The grimace on her face was about as bad as he'd ever seen it, reminding him of a summer party, where she'd opted to wear similar footwear. Just like tonight, she'd tried on the shoes again after a night of dancing, and instead of trying to walk in them again, she'd chosen to walk barefoot across the parking lot to the car.

But this time, there was an edge to her expression. Determination.

"Give me a second," she said.

He smiled, reaching for the glass of water the bartender passed in his direction. "No judgment."

She raised an eyebrow. "I didn't think you were judging me."

He could tell from the look in her eyes that she was remembering the same night he was. "I don't think you've changed so much since that walk in the parking lot." He took a drink of the water. Ice cold and perfect on his tongue. "I didn't judge you then, and I am certainly not judging you now."

"But you were going to ask."

"I didn't ask you then if you were going to wear the shoes and I'm definitely not going to ask you now. Your feet, your choice."

But as if she'd decided something else entirely, she reached out for a hand. He gave it to her, wrapping her fingers in his, feeling the heat of her touch. He supported her as she slid down the stool, landing on those heels.

He watched, transfixed, as she kicked out her feet, shaking an ankle and checking her balance.

She let his hand go and took a few steps before looking up again, and *he knew.*

He just knew what she was going to do as she stepped out of the shoes, leaving them on the ground behind her.

"Did you bring another pair?" he asked.

"No. I figure you deserve to witness a repeat performance."

He laughed, and it had been so long since he'd been able to laugh like this, carefree, with the look in Anna's eyes egging him on. If he could spend the rest of his life like this, he'd be a happy man.

"You two heading out?" Tony asked.

He forced himself back to reality, glancing at Anna as she stood, ethereal and gorgeous, barefoot and happy. "Whenever she's ready to go," he said. "Unless you need me for something?"

Tony shook his head as Charlotte emerged from the back. "Get out of here," she said, grinning. "Tony and I will take care of whatever needs to be done. I already kicked Ken and Rivvy out."

And as he and Anna headed toward the door, saying their goodbyes, he couldn't believe he'd gotten this chance.

≫≫≫✳≪≪≪

THE CAR JACOB took them to wasn't the convertible.

It was something else, a black sedan, the epitome of understated luxury. But as if it were yesterday, Jacob threw his jacket in the back seat and settled into the driver's seat. "You okay?"

Mostly. But she wasn't sure if she could tell him that. Not yet anyway. "I think so."

"Thirsty? If you reach down into the glove compartment, I've got a bottle of water."

She shook her head. "Not thirsty."

"Mmm?"

She'd heard a ton of his words, listened to a ton of his sounds, his laughs. That sound, with its very particular inflection, was a question he didn't want to ask but couldn't help himself.

But what was bothering her wasn't something she could or did want to answer briefly on the way to her grandmother's house.

He stopped at the light at the center of town, the halfway point between the party and home. She was running out of time.

Why couldn't she find the words? Why couldn't she just say it? Why couldn't she just tell him she wanted to talk about what had happened back in December?

"It's fine," he said, as if he'd misinterpreted her silence as an answer all its own. "Never mind. No worries."

"No. That's not it," she said. "I'm trying to figure out how to say this, not that I don't want to tell you."

"Okay."

That was genuine, like the look in his eyes, like the way she felt when she was with him. But when she looked out the window, she saw the familiar paint and landscape of her grandmother's house.

The sound of him unlocking the car meant she had really lost her chance.

Except...did it have to?

"Do you have to be anywhere?"

He raised an eyebrow. "Not really," he said. "I thought you wanted to go home."

She shook her head. "No," she replied. "I don't. Not now. What I want...what's wrong is that...I want to talk. Somewhere. Can you pick a place?"

His eyes lit up, and she felt the engine come to roaring life under her seat. The song playing on the satellite station was similar to one of the pieces they'd danced to earlier at the party. But this version was acoustic, slower.

She lost herself in the feeling of being with him as he

continued to drive. Past the buildings, past the Historical Society and the business district, into the backroads of the town beyond the high school. Away from everything.

Only when he stopped the car in the bits of gravel people had turned into an impromptu parking lot did she recognize where he'd taken her: the one place in town where they could see the water away from the marina and the downtown business district.

It was many things, the high school make-out spot being one of them, but more importantly, it was *their* spot. He'd taken her here so many times throughout their relationship. He or a driver assigned to him or her grandmother. Their last teenage summer, he'd made it a point to drive her here himself.

Instead of breaking the silence, she met his eyes with her own. It was powerful, the expression there in the depths of ocean blue. Wanting and recognition and something else that sat at the edges.

"Do you want to get out?"

"Yeah," she said. She couldn't stall anymore. "I'm ready." And so they headed toward the bench, her bare feet on the pathway. She wanted to hold his hand, but she couldn't. Not yet. Instead, she grabbed the fabric of her dress as they sat down.

She swallowed, took a deep breath.

"So what happened?"

His expression was pensive, slow. "I just want to make

sure. You mean in the city? Back in December? In front of the Grove Hotel?"

Of course he knew what she meant; he could always tell. When she didn't have the right words, he always did. He was better at reading her than anybody else on the planet, especially when the question was important. Like when he'd found out she'd gotten into grad school. "Yeah. You were as cold as an ice cube."

"I broke the rule," he said, his voice low. "The one cardinal rule between us."

I will always see you.

Uttered at eight, uttered at ten, uttered at thirteen and at fifteen. No matter how busy, no matter what, and he broke it. "So what happened? Is there an explanation?"

She could see him pulling the story together as he sat there. Not out of thin air but out of memory and context. Explanations mattered to him, even when his sense of scheduling didn't.

"My father's investment advisor was awful," he began, "and I wanted to tell him that his services were no longer needed after my father died, but...my father left me a series of tasks. Letters."

He paused again. "One of them was 'give Blake one more chance.' And so I kinda had to. The project, the chance Blake offered me, seemed like a good idea on paper."

"I don't understand."

"I did my due diligence, I looked between the lines as I

always do. The project ended up being a hot, steaming mess."

The phrase sounded strange coming out of his mouth for many reasons, and she couldn't help but laugh. "A hot mess, huh?"

She could see the shadows in his eyes. "I can't even tell you how bad it was."

"Bad circumstances? Bad people?"

He ran a hand through his hair. "Both. The gist of it was comprised of waspy schmucks trying to take advantage of zero financing. You know the type."

She did.

"People who never learned the meaning of the word no, who spend their lives drinking smug martinis at the right clubs, unaware of the systemic advantage that came with it, insisting when challenged that they deserve more of an advantage."

"Sounds worse than a hot mess."

"I can't go into details, but the bottom line is that all of them were awful, horrible people. They'd set a public meeting, to do what I think was an incognito photo op with me."

"Couldn't you just have stayed away and avoided the meeting and them? Sent them a 'it's not you, it's me' text?"

"No. I tipped off someone at the SEC that this was happening and sweetened the deal by pointing out that one of the guys who was going to be at that meeting had made a few insider trades. Enforcement was going to show up to chat with them, so I had to be there."

"So that explains your presence outside the hotel. What about the rule? What happened?"

He shoved his hands into his pockets, blew out a breath and stood for a brief second before he sat down. That was a tell; whatever he was going to say was something he'd wanted to protect her from. "So. Insider trading wasn't the only thing that was going on."

"Dammit, Jacob," she said. "Just say it, please."

"The guy who was with me was Christopher Hayward." He shuddered.

Definitely bad. "Tell me," she said. "What, why?"

"He'd had at least three rape charges shoved under the table. I didn't want you anywhere near him, and I especially didn't want him to pick up how much you matter to me. And so I did the only possible thing I could."

Now what he'd done made sense. In terrifying, technicolor clarity. "You made me believe you didn't care."

He swallowed, gulped in air as his voice shook. "I tried. He believed me, which was good. So good. But you did, too."

"Which wasn't so good."

"It was horrible."

Anna could see the pain in Jacob's eyes. He'd fallen on his sword to keep her from being run over.

He'd faced the consequences, and she did the only thing

she could. She held out her hand. "Never again?"

"Not without notice," he said. "I'll give you index cards."

She raised an eyebrow. "What?"

"Descriptions of people to avoid when they're with me," he said, shrugging. "Part of being so eminently believable is knowing that you're one of the few who can make sure the worst of society's criminals pay for what they do to others, you know? Forcing them to catch justice instead of allowing them to use their position as a way of avoiding consequence. So encountering these people will always be a part of my MO, my life. But I'll make sure you know."

"Aaaah." Yep. If she was going to be around him as an adult, she was going to have to be able to deal with the avenging part of his personality. "Okay. And you'll always warn me, as well as inform me?"

"Whatever I know that will help you," he replied, "I'll tell you." He paused and looked up at her. "No matter what that is."

And as if it were an olive branch, he took the hand she offered.

There were still problems they had to solve, things they had to face. But the way his hand felt around hers, the familiar warmth of his fingers, was everything she needed.

THERE WAS NO other explanation for the pure, giddy

adrenaline that flowed through Jacob's veins.

Something that had been coloring all of his interactions, all of his actions, weighing him down for the past five months showed signs of not just being fixed, but being repaired.

Anna's friendship, her presence in his life was so very crucial, and almost losing it had been as if he'd lost some vital part of himself. And now? Well, he wasn't out of the woods, but he was on his way.

And he was already trying to figure out what he could do to make them better. What was their problem before? Priority, trust. Schedule.

He needed to be there for her, and he needed to figure out how.

But in order to do that, there was one thing he needed to deal with first. There was a letter he needed to open. And so instead of heading upstairs to bed, he headed into the office. Sure, clear steps, following the path he took at least three times a day when he was at Rockliffe. The door opened easily and he walked in, over the carpet he crossed many times a day.

He stopped in front of his desk, staring at it.

It was, of course, the same desk he stared at when he was working at Rockliffe, but this time there was a degree of importance to what he was doing. He blew out a breath and sat down, opening the drawer where he'd kept that letter.

The paper was cream-colored and gave under his fingertips. He reached for his father's letter opener and used it to cut through the back of the envelope, like he had with the others. A flick of his wrist and it opened, quicker than the others.

The emotions were intense enough that he needed a moment before he read the letter. He put the envelope down on his desk. Took a few steps away and a deep breath, confronting the possibilities that could be contained in that envelope.

And when he was ready, he reached inside and removed a single piece of parchment, the letter in painstaking calligraphy.

This is the last task I leave you.

There are records in the archives of the treatment your grandmother sought and received for alcoholism. My thought and my expectation is that you will find and then remove them.

I understand that your relationship with her was difficult. I realize that she wasn't the best and didn't treat you or Anna with understanding.

But I beg you, Jacob.

Judge her for her personality, judge her on the way she treated others, especially later in her life. Your grandmother does not deserve to be judged, by you, for this.

Your Father

Jacob blew out a breath, his good mood evaporated in seconds.

This would be difficult, but it needed to be done in a way that didn't disturb Anna's work; this had nothing to do with the task she'd been asked to do. And whether or not he had good feelings for his grandmother, she deserved this.

Chapter Twelve

THE FIRST THING Anna smelled on Sunday morning was coffee. She walked downstairs, almost on autopilot, driven by her nose.

"How did you sleep? Are you hungry?" her grandmother asked from the foot of the stairs.

"I slept well, for sure, but not enough. I might take it easy today, although I have to pick up a few things."

Her grandmother nodded. "You didn't answer the hungry part."

"I didn't, but I think I am."

Oma smiled back at her and led her into the kitchen. "I feel like some eggs and toast. You pour the coffee, and I'll make some breakfast. Maybe hash browns?"

She felt the rumbling in her stomach before she was able to answer. "I guess my stomach is answering for me."

Not long after, she and her grandmother were sitting at the wooden table in the dining room. She took a long sip of the coffee as her grandmother dished potatoes. "Oh, that is good," Anna said.

"I like cooking like this," Oma replied. "So how was the

party last night?"

"You don't mince words, do you?"

Oma smiled. "Nope. Not at all. I want to know what's going on."

Did she know what was going on? Did she know what to say?

She didn't. "I don't think there are easy answers," she finally said, starting with the truth. "The party was fun, and Jacob and I finally had a really good conversation. And even though it feels right again, we also have so much to deal with and I'm not sure if we'll be able to. Which makes me sad because it's so hard."

"It's hard when it's good, when it's important."

Anna took a piece of challah toast. "I think what's hard about it is, how intertwined we are and yet we're not…synched right now."

"Not synched?"

She nodded. "We had an incident a few months ago, and we finally talked about it, but now that we've dealt with this problem, how do we tackle what else is going on? How did we get to the point where this rule became easy to break, and a deal breaker? One that feels…insurmountable."

"Okay. So what else is happening? What's the problem?"

"Well." Anna sighed and took a bite of her eggs. "Aside from the mess with Jacob that colors the way I see Rockliffe Manor, my new friends expect me to be making life-changing decisions because my career happened to bring me here for a summer. They act like I've moved here."

"Well," her grandmother asked, "have you?"

"I haven't," Anna replied. "I'm still the same person, my apartment and job are both in the city, and my parents still live in Hollowville. I'm just on a special assignment. People do that and come back. How do I get them, all of them, to understand that?"

"Friendships are complex things," her grandmother said.

"Tell me about it." It occurred to Anna that of all the people in her life, her grandmother was best equipped to talk to her about the nature of friendships. "Speaking of friendships, what's the story with you and Rose? How did the both of you get so close?"

"Rose and I are friends," her grandmother replied after a fortifying sip of her coffee, "because she needed someone who didn't care about who she was. Someone who was a Rockliffe Manor resident because of the town, not because of the Horowitz-Margaretens. At the Jewish Center, in the community, they never know who they can trust. Heck, in the wider world, they have to be careful. They need safe places here, too."

Anna swallowed some more coffee and smiled back at Oma. "Thank you," she said. "That does make a lot of sense. And Mom?"

"What do you mean?"

"I mean how she fit in to," she gestured widely, "to Rockliffe Manor, to all of this."

"Aaaah. Well, your mother, and I love her, was more interested in the wider world than anything. Not Jacob's father and not the town, which she always likened to a feudal bit of ridiculousness. Hollowville isn't Rockliffe Manor. And she is very much happier there, I think. It's why your mother studied history, but ended up teaching ethics and public policy."

"I think it's probably why I study history, too."

"What?" Oma laughed. "You also think you're sitting in a dukedom?"

Anna shook her head. "Because I learned so much about Jewish history here, how integral Judaism was to the foundation of the town and the way it operates."

"Yep. The first Fredrick Horowitz-Margareten gave his famous middle finger and built Rockliffe. Makes sense." Oma smiled. "You take your coffee, and I'll clean up. Maybe take a breather in the living room."

She smiled. "I'll clean up next time."

"Good."

An offer this good wouldn't come around that often. She headed into the living room. She needed to email Jemima and let her know how things were going before her boss decided to check up on her. Not to mention, she needed to remind herself that her life was in the city, no matter what happened here in Rockliffe Manor. So she sat on the couch, drinking more of her coffee, and prepared an email that did just that, clicking past the reminder she'd left herself to talk to Jacob about the document she'd found.

JACOB WANTED TO hide in his office, or from the letter, but the schedule that was slowly becoming impossible to ignore wasn't going to let him, and so on Monday, he offered to bring Anna lunch.

He arrived at 1p.m. just outside the archives where she was waiting. "Let's go have a picnic," she said.

He took her hand and let her lead him through the grounds and the hills they'd rolled down as kids, the lake they snuck their feet into on the hottest of days, and the stone grotto where they'd eaten ripe fruit the housekeeper had gotten from a farmer's market.

That was where she'd wanted to sit.

And he found himself absolutely transfixed. This was the perfect place to eat lunch, a pastrami sandwich on rye, with mustard. Hers was tongue on white, of course, no rye or mustard anywhere near it.

Her eyes widened, joyful as she opened the wax paper package. "This is gorgeous. Perfect."

He smiled back at her, his mouth unable to do anything else. "You're welcome," he said.

"You remembered."

"How could I forget?" He basked in the joy of her expression before biting into his sandwich.

"So," she said after a while, "you've got a busy week?"

"Yeah. The email from my assistant doesn't necessarily make me feel better."

"What's your plan?"

He shrugged. "Don't know. I need to take care some of the minor fires, organize the things I was telling you about both here and in Texas."

"Texas?"

"Yeah. Few more things I need to oversee."

"I've got to get to Hollowville this weekend, and I'm going to back up the documents and start to get a sense of story. Which means I'll see you Monday."

He raised an eyebrow. "Huh?"

"You're going to Texas, I've got serious research to do, and I'm going to Hollowville. So I'll see you next week."

"Hollowville," he asked, just to make sure. "When are you going?"

"Probably leaving Friday, early. And I might have to take my grandmother's car because mine's acting up."

Her car was acting up?

No. He wasn't going to buy her a car or something dumb like that.

What did she need? What could he give her without obligation?

What part of himself could he offer her? Especially now. Especially when things were slow and new and starting on a different foot than they had before.

He was going to dive deep into the heart of why they hadn't worked before. He hadn't stood beside her, supported her, in places that weren't this one. If this was going to work, his support had to go beyond Suffolk County. If they were going to stick this time, he had to show her from the beginning. There was only one solution he had. One offer he could make.

"I'll drive you."

She raised an eyebrow. "You'll what?"

"I'll drive you," he repeated.

"How?"

"If it's something you want, it's possible." She didn't respond immediately, and so he continued. "You know if you don't want me to, I'll pull back, and you can forget I asked."

She shook her head. "You sound so busy as it is."

He smiled. "I'll leave tomorrow, be back from Texas on Thursday night. I'll sleep and pack a bag for the weekend and go with you."

"Weekend? I—"

"Were you planning on staying the weekend?"

She shrugged. "I don't know. I hadn't thought that far, but maybe."

"You have your parents, your friends there, right? People to catch up with?"

He could see the wheels turning.

"I do," she finally said, "I guess it would be nice."

"So," he said, carefully, casually, "either I'll drive you or

I'll get a driver."

"No."

What had he said to make her say no?

"I don't need a driver, Jacob. If you come with me, you drive. If this is going to be a thing"—she gestured to the space between them, the one he'd been actively trying to close—"then we don't need a driver for a quick trip to Hollowville."

He nodded, relieved. "Okay. No driver then. So we leave on Friday to avoid the traffic on the expressway."

"And the highway and maybe the bridge, depending on how ridiculous the route is."

He laughed. They'd taken so many ridiculous routes on the island, together, on a summer days, getting lost, eating pie, taking pictures of sunflowers. "Right," he said. "So we avoid all the traffic and I drive."

"And whatever you drive," she said, caution and warning in her tone, "make sure it's comfortable to sit in, easy to park in Hollowville."

He had choices, but one stuck in his mind. Clearly. "Okay. I can do that."

"Good." She smiled. "I'm looking forward to it."

And more than he could say, he was too.

ANNA NEEDED TO get her head together. Which meant as

soon as she got back to her grandmother's, she initiated a Tikkun Online LivePic chat with Batya. "So," she said as her friend answered the call. "You going to be in Hollowville over the weekend?"

"Possibly."

Which was a good answer but not the one Anna really wanted. "That's fine. You're busy?"

"Finishing up a project so I can come to Rockliffe in June."

Anna settled back in her chair. "Well, I'm coming this weekend to look at some frames and pick up some things. But Jacob wants to come, so he's driving me."

"Driving you?"

She told the whole story, and adjusted her headphones as Batya stared.

"You're kidding."

She shook her head. "'Fraid not. And the thing is, I'm kinda excited for him to come to Hollowville, you know? To see what he's like there."

"Interesting. So you took your baggage to the cleaners?"

"We're starting to. How this incarnation of us plays out will depend on him. We need to fix the problems before we decide what this version of us is."

"Makes sense," Batya said. "A relationship that relies on things two kids did when they were little won't last longer than it takes to figure out the circumference of a lollipop."

Anna snickered. "Basically. If we get back together, it's

because of who we are now. Because of how we are now."

"Speaking of who you are now, have you and he talked about your job?"

She bit her lip. "Not about my boss, not since I saw him at the bar. He doesn't like her, but he trusts me, and that's about as far as it's gone."

"You know that's going to come up. You're not going to be able to avoid it forever."

She blew out a breath. "I think part of the reason I haven't brought it up is that I agree with him about Jemima. But I don't have the leverage to say anything or do anything about it, and even though I trust him to not do something, I just don't want to tempt fate. Besides."

Batya raised an eyebrow. "Besides?"

"My goal isn't to get fired or get Jemima fired. My goal is to put on exhibits that feature Jewish people doing things history erased. Standing up for those who needed help. And I am so very close to getting there."

"I have to get back to this project I'm in the middle of if you want me to get to Rockliffe Manor before next year, but before I go, I have to tell you something."

Anna smiled. "What is it?"

"Remember that the MMJH is only one of the places where you can put exhibits together. Don't get so devoted to the place that it overpowers the reason you went there in the first place."

Anna nodded, letting her friend's words sink in. "I adore

you, by the way."

"I know." Batya grinned. "Have a good weekend. Call me before Sarah does."

"I will!"

Anna ended the video chat. So much to think about. And not much time to do it.

Chapter Thirteen

THE WEEK MOVED quickly, filled with research and fun and all of the things she was starting to love about this stay in Rockliffe Manor. But Anna found herself staring at a text from Jacob early Friday morning, having just gotten dressed and dried her hair.

Tell me when you're ready and I'll drive over.

She still didn't know why he'd insisted on coming to Hollowville with her. She'd thought he'd overschedule and buy her a train ticket, like he had in the past.

But he didn't. He hadn't overscheduled himself. He'd chosen, and made this trip a priority.

She headed to the kitchen, brought her bag and poured herself a quick coffee and texted Jacob back.

Whenever you're ready.

Her phone rang shortly after.

"Is this a 'whenever you're ready' and you're not ready yet or a 'whenever you're ready' and come over now?"

His voice sounded scratchy, as if he'd been the one who'd just woken up, which made her laugh for some reason. "Closer to the latter. I'm drinking coffee, dressed and ready to go. So whenever you get yourself here, I'll walk out the door."

"Okay."

"Seriously though." She paused. "You sound tired. You don't have to drive to the other side of the state if you don't want to."

"I'll see you in ten minutes."

And as he hung up the phone, she found herself trying to figure out what this moment between them meant. What road were they on now? What was their destination?

Her view through the window on a May morning didn't hold any answers, and neither would her sleeping grandmother. And the reminder note on her phone to talk to him about the document she'd found when researching wouldn't tell her anything either.

She headed into the living room; the car Jacob had driven her home in from the party only a week before was in front of the house.

His smile was slow and sleepy as he stood on the porch, his eyes bright on top of the dark circles engrained in his face.

"You look exhausted."

He shook his head. "I had a good sleep last night, and I slept on the way home. So I'm fine. I keep promises I make."

She folded her arms and picked up her tote bag, and the handle for her rolling bag. "Look, I…"

A familiar expression flashed across his face; there was

something he wanted to say but he couldn't, or wouldn't. But once his expression had settled, he said, "It means something that you asked—er, let me escort you."

"But what does that mean?"

He shrugged. "I guess it means whatever you want it to."

"So where does that leave us?"

"Instead of telling you," he said, looking at her as if he were about to break, "I'm going to show you. I'm going to keep my promises and go with you to the small town I've heard about intermittently for years but have never been to."

"You've never been?"

He shook his head, then paused. "I haven't been with you."

Which made sense. Hollowville was hers, just like Rockliffe Manor was his. He'd never met her parents, never eaten at the Caf and Nosh with her. Which meant he'd never seen Hollowville the way she knew it.

"Okay. I get it."

"So you're ready?"

His smile could light the sun. There was adventure in his eyes. And there was nothing else she could do but nod. "Yes. I'm ready," she said.

And because she was feeling charitable, she let him take her bags and put them in the trunk. She also let him open the passenger door.

"I could get used to this," she said.

The dimple showed in his smile. And as he walked

around to the driver's seat, she thought she heard him say, "It's what I'm hoping."

She wasn't sure how she wanted to react to that, but it was a sign she was going to be in serious trouble. Resisting Jacob when he was like this was impossible, and right now, as she sat in the car next to him, the clear fact was that she didn't want to.

JACOB COULDN'T BELIEVE his luck. It was a Friday. Yes, there was traffic on the LIE, but the sky was clear, and he had a cup of coffee and most importantly, Anna. There was nothing else he wanted in the world.

He was more than ready to see Hollowville, maybe casually meet her parents. In fact, this visit was way overdue.

"You're okay with staying with my parents?"

Her comment came out of nowhere. Thankfully, he'd had years of experience holding himself tight, which kept the car on the road. There were hotels in the area, one part of a chain that had a pretty big business. But all the same, he nodded.

"Yeah," he said.

She grabbed another sip of coffee as he watched her out of the corner of his eye.

"You sure you're okay with not only meeting them, but staying over? I mean, it's a lot."

"It's fine," he said. He had to be careful. He wanted to know what to expect, what he'd be facing, but he didn't want to make her nervous. "Do they have opinions about us, about me?"

Anna sat back against the leather seat and closed her eyes. "Dad, not so much, not really. Mom on the other hand? She likes Hollowville because of 'the way it is.' She thinks Hollowville seems a bit more egalitarian than Rockliffe Manor."

Egalitarian. "No family like mine in the center?"

"Exactly."

He knew that a family like his made small-town life more difficult than it should be at times. People in the manor were closer knit, gossip was quicker, and outsiders were distrusted more so than others, even though some of the townies caused just as much trouble.

"On the other hand, she did grow up with your father."

Yep. The bump and rush that came with living in and growing up in a small town stayed with people forever. There was no telling how Anna's mother would react to him, there in her house, with her daughter. But what could he say that would mitigate or prepare Anna for the idea that her mother wouldn't like him on principle?

"Jacob?"

He blew out a breath and just went for it. "My father was many things. A good father, for starters, but there are people who believe what you leave behind is much more important than what you do to deserve it."

"Legacy can be a weight or a buoy."

"My grandmother complicated matters," he said, whether to himself or her he wasn't sure. "She believed position mattered so much more than who you could help. There was a reason," he said, carefully, "that your grandmother and my mother needed to find common ground so quickly."

"What did your grandmother think about us?"

His grandmother and her politeness lessons had worn on him after he'd spend a few moments of freedom helping those who were wronged by years of systemic injustice. He wasn't going to tell Anna that. "I think by the time she felt comfortable enough about expressing her opinions in front of me, she realized that they didn't matter. I was the son, the only child. She couldn't jeopardize her relationship with me while there was a chance I'd be in control of her future." *And,* he thought, *her legacy.*

Anna's smirk was a thing of beauty. "She hated the idea of 'us,' huh?"

"Putting it mildly, yes."

"So my mother hated your father, my grandmother wanted to save your mother from both your father and your grandmother, your mother wanted an ally and a friend who sat outside your bubble, hence the conspiracy at the palace?"

He laughed. There were documents and documentaries that had a habit of calling Rockliffe a palace, and though he understood the reasons, he'd never been comfortable with the word. "I wouldn't call it a conspiracy, but I'd call it some kind of plan. I don't know what their master plan was then. I definitely don't want to know what it was now."

"Same."

He nodded, focusing on the road, on the way it curved and bent.

"This is the exit," she said as he'd come out of what felt like a hairpin turn. "Welcome to Hollowville."

><>>><<<<

ANNA HAD JACOB pull into a parking spot in the lot across from the bookstore. It was just before lunchtime. "So what do you want to do?"

He grinned at her as he got out of the car. He looked like a kid in a candy store, bright eyed and ready to take on the world. "I'm an open book," he replied. "I'm ready to see everything you want to show me."

And just as easily, inspiration struck. She'd finished the book she'd been reading and she needed another. Tales from Hollowville had to be the first stop. She didn't have to meet Sharon Rosen-Perez at the art store until later in the afternoon, so they had time. Bookstore, lunch at the Caf and Nosh, and finally the art store. If she could hold herself together until then. With Jacob.

"Okay," she said, as he locked the car before taking care of the parking fee. "How much time do we have?"

"I maxed it out because I wasn't sure how long we were going to need the space," he replied in a way that was so very Jacob she wanted to sigh.

"It's fine. Gives us more time before we have to move the car."

He nodded, carefully. "Okay."

And because he seemed genuinely nervous, she offered her hand. "It's really fine. I'm glad you're here."

And with those words she could see his shoulders drop a little and his posture loosen just a bit more. "Me, too."

Hand in hand they headed to the stairs. For the first time in their entire relationship, she was with Jacob just to be with him outside of Rockliffe Manor. Where her business was the reason they'd left Long Island, bypassed the city and came into Westchester. Where the pressure and the attention was on her.

Where nobody was really watching him, he could just be the curious, brilliant, funny Jacob she'd always known. The Jacob without the weight of history on his shoulders.

"I like this," he said, half dreamily. Not just once, but a record seven times in ways she could interpret because she'd been around him long enough. The smells, the architecture, the feel of Hollowville.

She gestured as she opened the door of the bookstore, and she couldn't help but smile as his eyes widened at the smell of the books.

He looked at her as if he were pleading, so she let his

hand go, letting him head off to explore. She watched happily as he a made beeline to the business section. Once he was settled, she headed off to the romance section, of course. Her best friend had made a lot of progress on the floor. So many more books, so many more authors Anna wanted to read but hadn't had a chance to.

Except this wasn't a random adventure. She grabbed a few of Melanie Gould's books and the anthology Penina Alton-Schrader had talked about in February when Anna had seen the two authors for Galentine's, and then she went to find Jacob.

He was, of course, standing in front of the history section, holding a stack of books he'd picked up from a few different sections, including, of all things, the book by Penina Alton-Schrader she'd just finished, and a book by Miriam Greenberg about the T'ruah Awards.

She picked up her own stack, grabbed Katie Feldman's latest cookbook, and pointed to his. "Very cool."

He pointed at the Miriam Greenberg. "Her brother's Jake Greenberg, VP at Tikkun Online."

"That's interesting. But why the book?"

"She's been following the fledgling Jewish Music Association for years before it became mainstream. I've been waiting for this one."

If she was going to be around him more regularly, she'd have to get over the fact that he was getting book recommendations from the higher-ups at Tikkun Online.

"But what about this one?" she asked, pointing to the Penina Alton-Schrader and brandishing the anthology.

"Well," he said with a grin, "great minds think alike. I've read Penina Alton-Schrader's brilliant book about the founding of the British stock market, and when I read an interview where she said she was going to go back to writing romance, I figured I'd give this a try."

"Good reasoning. She's one of my favorites. If you like it, you can borrow a few of mine. I, on the other hand, actually need to read the book about the stock market."

"You can borrow mine if you like," he said before he turned his attention to her stack of titles. "She's doing some really great work with her Helping Hands Foundation, following the tradition of some great chefs," he said, pointing at the cookbook. "And I think Melanie Gould and her husband are doing some amazing things with the Empire Bridge Foundation. Not that it's theirs, of course, but her husband plays for the Empires and it's the team's charitable arm."

She smiled. "You amaze me," she replied.

A flush slowly made its way across his cheeks. "No," he replied. "I'm not exactly someone who should be the target of your amazement. It's these people, on the field, rolling up their sleeves. Not me. Not at all."

"And that's one of the many reasons I adore you."

She went back to shopping, going back to fill the holes in her collection of Penina Alton-Schrader's backlist before heading to meet Jacob at the cash register. Of course, he tried to pay a minimum of three times, and she let him buy her the cookbook. She was too proud of herself for not buying all of Melanie Gould's backlist to care about what Jacob was doing.

Except she couldn't help but watch as he took the last few pieces of paper from the book wish list.

"You don't have to do that."

He looked at her, half nervous, half embarrassed. "Do what, exactly?"

She pointed to the slips of paper. "Do that."

She saw the gears in his head move as he tried to figure out how to answer. "Call it a…I don't know, a habit, a reflex, a moral imperative."

Of all the people, it would be Jacob to say something like this. "You can't help yourself."

He shook his head. "No. I can't."

And because she knew him, she nodded. It wouldn't be him any other way. And it was him she was starting to realize she needed more in her life.

JACOB WAS A bit overwhelmed, but happily so. It just felt right being here with her.

"You hungry?"

"Very much so."

"I have a plan," she said, her smile bright. "Follow me."

He wanted to say *anywhere* but she'd probably balk at that. Instead, he followed her down the street, through what had to be the town's business district. Chocolate shops, a knitting store, a grocery store, and a café.

The café held the corner space, large, blue and white subway tiles and a sign proclaiming the name: The Caf and Nosh.

Anna stood on the sidewalk, almost frozen. What was wrong?

"You okay?"

She straightened her jaw and her shoulders, as if they were going into battle. "So," she said. "This is…"

He raised an eyebrow. "A meaningful place? A scary place?"

"A place that knows the town gossip."

Each town had that one place the community gathered. "They come here after Shabbat services?"

"Best Saturday brunch ever. If you're going to be in Hollowville with me, you need to eat here."

With me.

The two most important words in the entire sentence. He'd do anything to be with her. Anything she asked him. And so he braced himself, not for him but for her, and held out his hand for her to take. She did; it didn't even take a second.

Holding her hand as they walked into the café felt comfortable, as if her touch was the visible sign of approval he needed, that or he was reveling in the simple feeling of being grounded by the warmth of her fingers. Either way the familiarity grounded him as they walked past the threshold into the café.

No sooner had they stepped inside, was he hit by a cloud of fantastic scents and smells. Of matzah brei and whitefish and lox, of coffee and of cream soda.

"This smells wonderful," he said.

She smiled shyly, and as he was about to ask her what was going on, he heard the sound of plastic against wood as the menus dropped on the tables.

But none of the people who were suddenly empty handed, were looking at him. He'd spent his life under a microscope. And the expressions on the faces of the patrons here weren't any he'd ever seen directed at him.

They were looking at Anna. She was the local, the one everybody watched. The one whose welfare mattered. To them, he was an intruder. And so they inspected the way her hand sat happily and comfortably in his, the way she led him into the restaurant, standing her ground, smiling. All of that mattered to these people.

"Anna, how are you?"

"Fine, Chana." She gestured toward Jacob. "We need a table for two."

He smiled. The older woman with the short, black hair seemed proprietary over everything; either this was her restaurant or she thought it was.

When she met his eyes, he could see the judgment, but not the same way people in Rockliffe Manor or Manhattan did it. "Of course," Chana said in a very clear Israeli accent, "the mensch who bought out the book wishes gets to sit with you."

Now he understood why Anna had pointed out the gesture he'd made at the bookshop. In most small towns, gestures like that one were noticeable. And the very last thing he wanted in general was any form of notoriety for things he felt were important.

"Gossip travels like lightning here."

"You, *yaldah*, are a member of this community even though you don't live here," Chana said, smiling at Anna even as she tried to look at anybody but him. "You're someone who matters to us here in Hollowville. And it's a good thing your gentleman has a good heart," she added to Anna.

Which he figured was about as big a seal of approval as he'd get.

"Now sit, order, and let me feed you, hmm?"

And instead of having the extended conversation he'd expected, Anna steered him to the table, the one he'd have picked himself. He settled in for a good lunch.

"This is Hollowville," Anna said, and he felt her hand over his across the table.

But she sat up straight and swallowed as the door swung

open.

What was happening? "Is everything okay?"

"Yeah. It's just...prepare yourself for what's about to happen. It's not bad, but it's not going to be as organized as I expected, okay?"

"Okay." She'd be able to take him anywhere, do anything with him, and he'd understand. "It'll be fine," he said, "whatever it is."

ANNA COULDN'T BELIEVE her life.

Well. She could except for the fact that her head had just exploded.

She was sitting across from Jacob in the Caf and Nosh, and Sarah, who they were going to see later, had just walked in, Isaac on her heels. She'd hoped to talk to Jacob more about her friendship with Sarah, tell him how it had changed in the last six months, and warn him about how protective her best friend had become before seeing her, reintroducing them. Yet here she was.

Now there was no going back. No return. The two most important people in her life were meeting again and her heart pounded hard against her chest. "Hey, Sar," she said quietly.

She held her breath as Sarah made a beeline for the table, Isaac right behind. And as had happened a million times before, Anna stood and put her arms around her best friend.

"Oh my God, Anna. Oh wow."

Anna could easily pinpoint the exact moment in time where Sarah looked over her shoulder and saw Jacob.

"So is this version of Jacob on the good list or the bad list?"

Anna smiled, hoping they'd both take a cue from her mood. "On the good list."

"And you intend to stay there, right?"

"I do," Jacob replied, taking it seriously as she hoped he would. "It's important that we figure out how I stay there, and what I need to do."

Sarah raised an eyebrow. "We?" Anna met her best friend's eyes, and saw understanding there. "Interesting. In any case," she continued, "I'll be watching you."

Anna grinned as Jacob nodded, the serious look still in his eyes. "I expect no less. Anna deserves good friends."

The weight came off her shoulders, and the tantalizing smells of the restaurant made her stomach growl with anticipation.

The group ordered together, of course. All of the best things: matzoh brei, challah French toast, noodle kugel, potato latkes, knishes…it was such a wonderful hodgepodge. Conversation was easy and light until it was time to pay the bill.

Anna patted Jacob's hand. She knew if he had his way, he'd pay, but she didn't want a fight of any kind.

He took her hand in his and smiled slightly. There was a bit of a strain in his eyes, but she squeezed his hand and the strain went away.

And when Isaac got up, Jacob went with him.

Out of the corner of her eye, Anna could see Jacob take out his phone, type a bit, and pass it to Isaac. There was a quiet, whispered conversation, Isaac holding the phone, pursing his lips.

"Do you know what's happening?" Sarah asked.

Anna shook her head. "No," she replied. "I haven't the faintest idea."

Sarah leaned closely across the table. "You okay?"

"I'm actually pretty good."

Sarah's nod made her smile. She was even happier with the smile on Isaac's face and the way Jacob kissed her cheek when they came back to the table.

"So what happened back there?"

Jacob smiled at the look in Anna's eyes as he pulled out of the parking lot, starting the drive to her parent's house. But his hands were sweating, and he tried not to grip the steering wheel too hard.

"Clearly," he finally said, "we both wanted to pay. I said if he let me, I'd give him a commission from the foundation."

"What commission?"

"The foundation's hosting the Summer Days Ball, right?"

"I thought so."

"Which, by the way, takes place the first night of Summer Days."

"By the way?"

She raised her eyebrow. He was horrible at being subtle, which is why he rarely tried, though why he thought trying now would be a good idea, he'd never know. "Anyway, the tradition is that the ball has a centerpiece, usually designed by a local artist." He grinned. "This year, nobody at the foundation or the ball committee, or even the festival committee, could agree on a centerpiece, and the Chamber of Commerce was no help."

"But Isaac isn't a local artist; he's not even from Long Island. He's from the city. Doesn't that take him out of the running?"

"Your best friend's boyfriend is a world-renowned sculptor, and the committee needs *something* to put at the center of the ball. I figured, why not combine the two? I mean, if the committee's going to agree, they might as well agree on commissioning someone like Isaac to make an appropriate sculpture."

"You know," she said, "that's two."

"What do you mean?"

"You were at the council meeting where they also moved

forward on Batya's contract? For the website?"

"I was at the council meeting."

"And did you inquire about the website?"

"Yeah," he said, trying to focus on the directions. "I did. Apparently, the contract had been mired in bureaucratic red tape. I just suggested they move it along."

She sighed in the way she did when she was seeing right through him. "Which means, that's two of my friends you've made somewhat sure are going to be at the festival next month."

He tried to look nonchalant, but he was worse at being nonchalant than being subtle. "Well," he managed, "I…"

"You're watching out. Making sure my Hollowville friends aren't kept out of my time in Rockliffe. Thank you."

He smiled. "I will. Always. Besides, it's important that your friends aren't kept out of your life."

"Here." She pointed to the driveway. "It's this one."

"Okay," he said as he pulled in. His stomach started to roil. *It will be okay.*

As he turned off the motor, she took his hand. "We'll be fine," she said. "I promise."

And despite everything, he believed her. Because there was no other alternative.

ANNA WAS ABOUT to lose her mind.

Her father, her brilliant horticulturist father, had kept conversation going. It was lovely. But her mother was another story. She was a professor, specializing in ethics and public policy. And Anna felt as if they were in class, as opposed to sitting down at Shabbat dinner. Apparently they were having the Socratic method along with the chicken and matzah ball soup.

She wasn't sure where they were headed, until her mother smiled at an answer Jacob had given and nodded pointedly. "So, Jacob," her mother said, "do you think it's possible for a billionaire to be ethical?"

Anna shook her head. "Oh wow," she began. "Can you possibly leave the classroom at school?"

Her mother smiled and took a sip of her wine. "It's an important question, I think. And if he doesn't want to answer, that's fine. No judgment, but these are important questions."

"It's fine," Jacob said, that look in his eyes he got when he was thinking about something as he turned to her mother. "I agree they're important questions."

There was something like surprise in her mother's eyes.

"Well, that's good to hear," her mother replied. "Have you thought about how you'd answer that question?"

He nodded, and Anna could see him relax. "Billionaires," he said, "are only ethical when they use their power and influence to correct the systemic injustice that has affected so many for so long. Once they stop doing that, they are no longer ethical."

"Interesting." She smiled, which was something Anna did not expect. "Do you hold yourself to that standard?" her mother asked, not batting an eye.

"I do."

Anna took a deep breath and relaxed into her seat. This was Jacob at his best. She'd seen him exhausted most of the time, yet his sole focus was making things easier for others. He never wanted the spotlight, never acted as if he'd deserved more space than anybody else. He did the work and forced the spotlight on everybody else.

She'd had trouble with so many things about him, but his moral compass and ethics were never on that list. If they had been, the first time they'd ended things would have been the last. Relationships didn't fix people who were morally broken.

But between dinner and dessert, her mother practically dragged her into the kitchen, closed the door behind them, and paced the length of the kitchen.

"I have to say, I'm surprised, Anna."

"What can't you believe, Mom?" she asked, quietly, calmly as she opened the drawer to take out the napkins.

"He's definitely not what I expected, I'll tell you that much. It's hard for me to see past what I know of his family, but I can *possibly* see what you see in him. He definitely isn't his father, for sure."

She'd never met Jacob's father; late nights at the office,

very carefully scheduled business trips, and very clearly defined times she was allowed over took care of that.

Which was why she and Jacob had their rule.

I'll always see you.

"He's a good guy," she said. "At least I think so."

"But I'm fascinated, really," her mother continued. "What has he been doing to alter systemic injustice? Do you know?"

She smiled as she folded napkins. "If you actually want to know, I can tell you," she replied, "but I'm not sure you really want to know."

"Not now," her mother replied. "But I'm not ruling that conversation out. I'm just glad you're seeing it. What I am more concerned about is that you don't get subsumed in him. He's larger than life, and I'm not sure spending your summers there prepared you for…what his life really is. You need a supportive partner, and no matter how big his heart is, I'm not sure he could be that."

Anna knew where her mother was coming from; her father was the rock in their family and in her parents' relationship. She'd spent her summers in Rockliffe Manor because it was easier for a professor to prepare, edit, and publish papers over the summers without a small child around craving attention. And that never would have happened or become tradition without the support of her father and her grandparents.

As a child she remembered how every single conversation

she had with her mother during those summers were distracted as work, papers, and everything else took up Mom's time. The only marked change happened when Anna started working at the Historical Society and her mother could find some common ground for the academic theories she was speaking about. She never questioned it; as an adult, she even understood it.

But this was not the conversation to have now. And as she decided how to answer her mother without losing her mind or her marbles, there was a creak as her father inched his way into the room.

"Helen," her father said as he crossed the room. "We should have dessert."

And the expression on her father's face was relaxed, his smile bright. The conversation was over. Because Jacob was there, sitting in the living room, waiting. She went into the room, sat down next to him on the small two-seater, and took his hand in hers.

Without saying anything, he put his fingers around her hand, soothing her with a touch as only he could. They had a distance to go, but they had a solid foundation and she could live with that.

Chapter Fourteen

JACOB STARTED THE long drive back to Rockliffe Manor feeling excited, exuberant. And he wanted to hold on to that feeling as long as he could because once they got back, reality would intrude in some shape or form.

And the letter still hung over his head.

"I think," Anna said after they'd been cruising for a little while, "you should have dinner with my grandmother at some point."

That was a very easy ask. "I love the idea of having dinner with your grandmother."

"Excellent." She paused, and he heard her phone beep as she sent something.

Although he hadn't meant immediately, if she'd sent a question for tonight, he wouldn't mind at all.

"Also," she replied, her eyes brightening as they hit traffic on the Cross Bronx, "one day you should show me around Rockliffe Manor, the way you know it. I want to see it through your eyes."

The idea of her being in town, seeing it the way he did? The culmination of plans he, Ken and Tony had brought to life? "I'm looking forward to it."

And the smile on her face could have made his year.

"And you're good with tonight?"

"More than," he replied. "I'm looking forward to it." Which was an understatement for sure. He couldn't wait to get started.

"And," he said to her grandmother as they walked inside, "you're sure that it's not too much trouble to have me for dinner?"

"I am, *tateleh*. I am very sure."

Jacob nodded; any kid who grew up in and around a household where Yiddish was a love language would understand the diminutive was bestowed only on welcome, beloved family. "Then I'm absolutely looking forward to it."

"Good," her grandmother said. "That's settled. You two come in, sit down, take a breath, and wash up. Set the table, Anna, and I'll take care of the rest."

And as her grandmother went into the kitchen, Anna put her arms around him, briefly, just briefly. He eased into her embrace before he stepped away.

"I wonder why she said tonight, you know?" he asked. "Do you think your mother called her?" he asked.

"Oh I'm sure," Anna replied, reaching out her hand again for him to take. "My strong and sneaking suspicion is that," she gestured widely at the space between them, "this is her hope. You and I seem to gravitate toward each other and have for years. And a relationship will work between two people who will always find their way home—or at least that's what she's said for the past however many years."

And all he had to do was finish the list his father had entrusted him with, which would help to pave the way for visions he was starting to have of the future.

Visions he'd always kept in the deepest part of his brain.

First this, then his scheduling, and his promises.

Anna was the most amazing part of his life; if things went as he dared to hope, he could visualize a future where he could ask her if she wanted it to be hers, too.

"What's in your head?" she asked, quietly.

"I'm glad we're talking about things that matter."

She smiled. "Well," she replied. "We're doing the work. We're learning about each other, trying to fix things we broke instead of just trying to follow the same patterns."

"I have so much I want to tell you," he said. "So much."

"I want to listen. There's also so much I want to tell you."

"I will listen," he said.

There was something in her eyes that he wanted to dive into, the way she and her grandmother made him feel as they sat down to dinner. Welcomed. Loved. And he wouldn't stop working to deserve that love.

"I'm glad you're here. First of all, Jacob, call me Celia, please. You're of an age where I always wonder who Mrs. Green is."

"Celia," he said, testing the name on his tongue, even

though it felt weird.

"I'm glad you accepted my invitation for many reasons. You're always welcome in my house, Jacob, at my table, whether you're with my Anna or not. And I'm glad to see you two together."

And he hoped it would stay that way.

ANNA HAD LONG suspected that her grandmother had been playing matchmaker but the confirmation almost made her choke on her soup.

"Don't be so shocked, *mamaleh*," her Oma said with a smile. "When Rose and I first spoke about the two of you being playmates, all I wanted was for you to have a friend. If you were going to spend long periods of time here, you needed a child your age to play with. As you got older, I had an idea of what I wished to happen. But it would be your life, your choices that would determine the course of your relationship. It seems you found each other."

Had they? Could this time be the one they found each other for good?

And what would that mean for her job prospects, her life? Her career?

Would she lose what meant the most to her once she and Jacob settled into the basics of a relationship?

She sighed, smiling at her grandmother and at Jacob.

"Jacob," her grandmother said, "you have a heart as big as the world, and it's hurting. You need to realize that we love you for the person you are, not what you do. And yes. It is important for you to do your part, but there are people who love you just because of you."

"There are," Anna said. Because it was true. And she needed to remind him that there were people like her in the world who cared about him, too.

"Thank you," he said before taking a bite of his kugel. "This was important. And I'm really enjoying dinner. Thank you for having me."

And after they'd had dessert, he walked her to the door.

"So I'll see you tomorrow?"

He shook his head. "Business in the city before flying back to Texas. Back in a few days for breakfast?"

She nodded. "I like that."

And when he brushed his lips against hers, she met them with her own. It was soft, sweet, the taste of the ice cream he'd eaten on his tongue.

It felt like home.

Yet long after he'd left, she sat with a glass of wine out on her grandmother's back deck. So much to think about.

Could she live here? Did she have to?

She didn't want to prove her friends right after all, and her job was in Manhattan. Her apartment was in Brooklyn.

She'd finish her work here, go back to Brooklyn, and then figure out the rest of her life. Right?

Right.

JACOB DROVE BACK to Rockliffe full of energy. Talking to Anna's grandmother over dinner reminded him of the importance of family.

Family was crucial, and his family deserved the best from him.

His best meant finally finishing the last task his father had set him, removing the document that detailed his grandmother's treatment from the archives. Once he completed it, the list would be done.

The list that had occupied him for two years. Finished.

He'd be free.

Free to start his own legacy for real.

It was dark as he pulled up the gravel-lined driveway to the archives, stopping right by the entrance.

He parked the car, punched in the code to the security system, and walked inside. This time, of course, the bright lights and high shelves didn't bother him.

But seeing the way the papers were organized did. He didn't want to touch them, not one.

He wouldn't put Anna's job in jeopardy.

Instead, he opened his phone and clicked to the file containing the map his father had drawn, taking careful steps along the cavernous floor. When he reached the file cabinet his father had indicated, he found a slim manila folder in the drawer.

Just like his father had described.

Except when he carefully removed the folder, there was nothing.

Where? Where could it be? Where could those papers have gone?

He wasn't going to stand here and open random drawers, grab boxes without the appropriate protective material or anything like that. He needed to be methodical.

He blew out a breath and continued to think, heading over to the desk area where…

The paper was separate, on the corner, waiting, silver staples clear against yellowing paper, untouched as if it had been forgotten.

And all he had to do was take it. Nobody would be the wiser. Nobody would know.

And so he took the folder, placed the paper inside, then closed the open drawer and left the archives, relieved.

The task was done.

He could go on with his life.

Chapter Fifteen

WHEN ANNA CAME into the archives the next morning, she went to the desk and noticed papers were strewn a bit.

Actually, something was missing.

An old paper she'd left out to show Jacob, a record that his completely sober, completely play-by-the-rules grandmother had needed and received treatment for alcoholism.

Which, considering how difficult that had been in those days, Anna was impressed, and whether it would affect his view of his grandmother, it was something he deserved to know.

But now the document was gone, her exhibit cards were out of place, and she was...

Breathe.

Breathe.

She needed to tell...someone.

Someone who wouldn't judge her. Someone who would help her figure out the mystery.

As if by memory, she pulled out her cell phone and dialed Jacob's number.

One ring. Two. Three.

She didn't think he'd answer, but she wanted to hear his voice on the recording, if nothing else.

"Hey," he said. "I'm just heading into a meeting. What's up?"

"Someone broke into the archives," she said, trying to keep her voice calm. "I...I don't know what to do."

There was silence on the other end. "Okay. I'll be there in an hour. It will be fine, I promise. Okay?"

His voice was a lifeline in the maelstrom; her hands shook, but listening to the calm in his voice, she could match it even if she didn't feel it. "Call me when you get here."

"I will," he said, sounding rushed. "I will."

The knot in her shoulders untied, lessening the tension there. She stood, started to pace. And tried to think of anything other than someone coming into the archives and stealing.

Eventually, finally, when she'd almost lost hope, her phone buzzed. "I'm here," he said.

He was a beautiful beacon, resplendent in a three-piece suit in the darkness of her fear. She didn't hold back but ran to him, throwing her arms around him, inhaling his scent and taking all the comfort his presence gave her before stepping back. "I know you can't stay," she said, staring up at him, "but I'm glad you're here. So what do I do?"

"What do you mean?"

"Is there a trip wire? Someone in the local police department to call if things like this happen? A private security company?"

He shook his head. "No. It's fine. I don't think it's anything."

"Why? Do you know what was stolen?"

"Not stolen," he replied.

"How do you know that?"

But as she asked the question, her heart sunk. The fear and concern clawed at her throat and started to shake her stomach.

"Because," he said, clearly and confidently, "I was the one who took the document."

Hearing the words was worse than anything she could think of. It felt like a betrayal.

"You took it?" she asked.

"I did," he said as if nothing was wrong with what he'd done. "It was sitting on the desk…and I took it."

He'd taken it, and hadn't seen fit to tell her. He'd gone into the archives between Thursday night and this morning, before they went to Hollowville or after they'd gotten back, and took it.

After she'd started to trust him again. He'd gone in and just removed it. Not even told her.

What if a card had been taken, what if something had been damaged?

Who would be blamed for it?

Who…

He didn't trust her enough. And that hurt. But she didn't walk away. Despite every single cell in her body screaming at her to leave and walk away, it was time to finish this.

"I HAD IT out because I wanted to talk to you about it."

Jacob had absolutely no idea what Anna was thinking. She was fascinated with his family's story, but this wasn't tied to the story she was telling. This had nothing to do with her work. It was only someone who'd treated her horribly when they were kids, someone whose history didn't matter to her.

"Why? So you could have a discussion about how horribly she treated us?"

"No," she replied. "Because I wanted to talk to you about how strong I thought she was. But I can't do that now because you waltzed in and took it. Do you realize how scared I was?"

"I'm here," he said, his heart pounding. He couldn't get the words out fast enough to reassure her. He reached for her, but she stepped just out of reach. He didn't follow. "I'm here, and I came as fast as I could. Because you were scared and I wanted to tell you what had happened."

"Why didn't you tell me before? Because, you know, there was a bigger, easier solution here. I didn't have to call you on the phone, terrified that someone had broken into my workspace, messed with your family archives and my cards. You could have trusted me."

"Your workspace? It is, of course, your workspace. But this is my family, not some abstract idea. I know you know that, but the closer strands of the documents relate to my relatives, not the relatives in names or in text or the ones you find in computer searches, but the ones I associate with, people I knew." He blew out a breath, wanted to pace but didn't want to turn his back on her. Not then, not ever. "It's their history I'm protecting. And this task? This was the last of the tasks my father trusted me with, asked me to take care of. It had nothing to do with you, nothing to do with your work or your space."

"You told me about your father's list," she said. "Why the hell didn't you trust me enough to tell me about this?"

"Because you'd get involved," he said. He needed her to understand; he needed her to get this. "This was mine to take care of, not yours. This wasn't something to burden you with."

"Burden? What kind of burden? You told me about the list. You. Sat. At. My Grandmother's. Dinner. Table. Where we talked about family and about how important it was. You could have told me. Last. Night."

"This was something I had to do, something *I was asked to do*, for my family," he said, carefully and clearly. She had to understand. "This had nothing to do with you and I didn't want you to be involved."

"Except I'm the one who would have been blamed if something had happened to anything in that building. I'm the one who you don't trust enough to tell anything. After all of this time, you don't trust me."

"I trust you." He swallowed. "I trust you more than life itself."

"But you don't act like it," she said, her eyes bright with tears. "You've never acted like it."

The alarm on his watch beeped. "I have to go," he said. "I have a flight…"

"You always have a flight. You always have to go." She sighed. "I don't know why I even try."

"Anna," he said. "Please."

"No. I thought you respected me, I thought you trusted me. I thought I meant something to you. But I'm just a waystation between commitments for you. I'm not real."

"You're everything," he said.

"Then prove it," she said. "Go to the airport. Leave. Because I can't deal with you right now. I can't deal with us right now. And if you stay any longer, I can't be responsible for what I do to you or to the shards of us."

And the only thing he could do, as his heart broke, was leave.

Chapter Sixteen

ANNA SOMEHOW MANAGED to pull herself together after Jacob left, treating the research like every single other project she'd done. This wasn't personal, she reminded herself like a broken record. It was business.

She had a job to do, a contract to fulfill, and an apartment to go back to in Brooklyn once this entire disaster was over.

This was, she reminded herself as she drove back to her grandmother's house, a means to an end.

But all the same she couldn't help but initiate a video chat with Batya once she'd settled in and put her pajamas on.

"I'm calling to check on the apartment," Anna said as she took a long sip of her tea.

"Likely story," Batya replied, grinning back at her. "Considering you're going to spend more time in Rockliffe Manor, hmm?"

Anna shook her head. "No," she said. "I'm not. That part of my life will be behind me once this exhibit is done."

"Behind you, huh?"

It was over.

A relationship that had defined most of her life was definitively and completely over.

Something broke inside her and she could barely get the words out. "It's over," she whispered, as if saying it louder would make it a lie. "I... He's... It's over."

"What happened?" Batya asked. "Tell me what happened."

And so, she told the story, the whole thing, the way he hadn't trusted her, the way he had left her behind and said, "He didn't think about what could have happened to my career if he damaged anything."

"I'm your friend," Batya said. "I adore you. If you want to hear advice, I can give you advice. If you don't want advice, I'm here just to be here."

Anna sat back against her chair, held the pillow, and sobbed. "I just... I don't know what to do. It's like something is missing, something important is missing, and I don't know how to fix it...but I don't know if I even want to."

Batya nodded. "Fair. That is very fair. But I think that you have to consider one simple fact."

"What is that?"

"You called him. He was in a meeting. You have no idea what that meeting was. He was back on the Island in an hour because you told him you were scared. He left whatever that meeting was because you needed him. An hour, door to door from Wall Street, all the way out there. Knowing what that traffic must have been."

"But he wouldn't have had to do that if he'd trusted me enough to tell me what he was up to in the first place."

"True." Batya smiled. "And yes. That's the crux of it. But all of the conversations you've had about him that I've heard? You focus on what he's not doing for you. And I know, there's a power imbalance and he needs to fit into your life. But in some ways, you also need to fit into his. And I don't know whether you've ever tried."

Anna started to think about the conversation she'd had with Jacob, the words that flew between them.

And what he didn't say.

JACOB PACED THE rented apartment in Texas. The blank walls, clear floors, and beautiful night he could see through the window gave him no answers.

He'd lost her.

Completely.

If he was in any way skilled with metaphors, he'd say that the empty apartment reflected the inside of his soul.

He'd never been so broken.

He sat down on the bed and pulled out his phone. Who could he call?

Not Tony, because this was date night and he wasn't busting into someone's date night with this.

Ken was the last person he wanted to discuss this with.

Which left *one* person he trusted enough to call. And that felt weird.

His circle was so small these days, even smaller now.

The person he felt comfortable talking to about something like this was someone he didn't want to disappoint further.

His mother.

Finally, he stared at the phone, and dialed her number.

Without waiting for her to answer he said, "I need help."

"Wait," his mother replied. "What actually am I hearing from you? Is everything okay?"

He shook his head. "Nothing is okay."

"What's wrong?"

"I'm sorry I've disappointed you," he said. "Over and over. I'm sorry I'm just not a good person, not in the way you deserve."

"What? Where is this coming from, Jacob? Your heart is as big as the world, but your problem hasn't ever been how good you are."

In the silence that rose, in the space where she expected him to answer her, he wondered what she was thinking and hoped she couldn't see through him.

But hope was fragile when dealing with one's mother, and if anybody in this world could read him, even when they weren't in the same room, it was her.

"What did you do, Jacob? What did you do that's eating you alive like this?"

"It's what I didn't do correctly," he replied. And despite his best wishes, because he couldn't help himself, he told his mother the entire story, how the task he'd been given by his father was simple, and he couldn't make Anna understand how important it was, and by doing it, he managed to almost mess up her work, and that he'd disappointed both her and Anna. And had lost Anna forever. "Make sure that she's okay," he said. "Her boss has been sniffing around again, and if you can…"

"I'm sorry, Jacob. I can hear your heart is breaking. But even now, you're not letting anybody in. You're not letting people see the inside of you, and I understand. I know it's hard to admit you're hurting or fallible, but you can't just hide."

"I have to be perfect," he said, holding himself together with pins and needles. "I can't make that kind of mistake because you…we as a people deserve better. And if I fall, they'll burn me in effigy."

"Oh, Jacob," she said, the words soft as a blanket, "you don't have to be perfect for anybody, let alone those who will always find fault, who have always found fault with who we are. Those who love you will always love you, messy, perfect, because it's you who matters. You need to let her in. You need to let *people* in."

And when he ended the call, he felt a little better, a bit less raw.

Maybe he could let someone in. Maybe he could fix

things.

Maybe everything wasn't lost.

Just because he'd cracked.

AFTER ANNA ENDED the call, she checked her email. She didn't expect anything new, but she caught up on a few newsletters she subscribed to and sent some inquiries about articles she'd seen.

Those simple actions started to help her feel a little bit more normal, as if she weren't in Rockliffe Manor but back in her apartment in Brooklyn, late at night before she was heading to bed.

But once she'd sent the last inquiry, she realized that she'd gotten a new email.

From Jemima: Rockliffe Manor Travel Plans.

Oh God.

She felt the dread down to her toes. It roiled in her stomach, made her hand shake.

And anything she'd thought about doing was now out the window. It was going to be a long night.

Chapter Seventeen

JACOB HADN'T SLEPT, and he could feel the sand in his eyes.

But he couldn't stay in bed any longer. So he got up and put a pod in the coffeemaker and set it up to start.

More caffeine would help. He hoped.

He had meetings today with some of the people he worked with at JIDS, getting more information about what they wanted for a policy arm as well as policy instruction. As he was going over his notes, his phone rang.

He flipped it over and took a look at the number. His mother. He picked it up.

"Hello?"

"I know you've got a busy day down there, but I wanted to let you know that Jemima Kellerman is coming to the house this afternoon. I've got a car meeting her at the train station, but I don't see this going well in the end for Anna."

"I can't intervene in Anna's situation. I don't want to cause her more trouble than I have already."

"Jacob." She sighed, as if reprimanding him. Maybe she was. "I understand why you think you can't intervene in

Anna's situation. But you're missing something here."

"What?" he asked, rubbing his eyes. "What aren't you telling me?"

"The problem is Jemima herself. You think she's horrible—you've been telling me as much for years."

"Well, she is horrible," he replied. "People have been talking about her for years."

"Talk, my dear boy, is cheap. If she ends up damaging the archives? You know who's been talking and where you can find proof that backs up those accusations, demonstrating how untrustworthy and how unemployable she is."

"But I…"

"Of course, if she's not as bad as you think she is," his mother continued, oblivious to anything he could say to the contrary, "you don't have to worry about Anna being caught in the middle, hmm? Because if Jemima causes damage and you don't want me to intervene on Anna's behalf, I won't be able to keep Anna from getting caught up in the maelstrom."

He hung up the phone, made a few notes, and braced himself to dive in.

⇢⟫⟫⟫⟨⟨⟨⟵

ANNA DIDN'T HAVE to pick Jemima up at the train station, so she did some research in the library before heading toward the house at three. Once she'd organized her papers, she stopped at her grandmother's house before heading over to

Rockliffe, dressing as if she were going to work in the city. Pencil skirt. Cardigan, heels.

Her makeup was perfect, a professional as best she could do.

She could handle this. It was her job.

But when she arrived at Rockliffe, Jemima was already chatting with Rose. "Oh, of course," Jemima said, her voice in that particular tone she used with anybody who had a lower status than her before turning back to Rose. "You'll have to forgive my assistant. She has no sense of time."

My assistant.

The tone reminded Anna of her role, of her position and her expectations. This was normal. This was fine. She was an assistant curator, and her boss was glad-handing a potential donor.

Because that's what this was, right?

It was no longer her, doing a project for a family she knew, in the town her mother was raised in and where her grandmother still lived. This was her job and Jemima was her boss. "Good afternoon."

Heads turned as if they were on a rotator, both Rose and Jemima suddenly looking in her direction as if she were nothing more than a germ.

"That is lovely, dear," Rose said in Jemima's direction, presumably about something they'd discussed before Anna had arrived. She didn't want to know.

"Oh, yes. Anna," Jemima interjected, "could you do me

a favor and get me a cup of tea? And I also want to see your progress on the index cards you've been putting together and preparing for my arrival."

The matriarch of Rockliffe simply nodded instead of adding any words into the ether.

If she'd expected better from Rose, Anna would have been disappointed. Instead, she took a deep breath and, as she'd done many times before, moved forward. "Of course, Jemima."

And if nothing else, the request was exactly what she needed to help her dive back into the role she usually occupied: assistant curator to Jemima Kellerman, with the exhibit of her dreams on the line.

Not Anna Cohen with a broken heart.

"So," Jemima said when Anna had returned with the tea, "I'd like to see what you're doing, but tomorrow, of course. I need my beauty sleep, and Rose has hired a driver to take me to my hotel. You will, of course, meet me at the archives, with breakfast."

"Breakfast?" Anna said, hoping her voice didn't shake. Jemima should know better, should be better at following the rules about document handling. "At the archives?"

"Well, yes," Jemima said. "I need my tea."

"I've been trying not to eat anywhere near the archives," she replied, desperately attempting to walk the line between being submissive and giving her boss a suggestion. "Or drink for that matter."

"Oh whatever." Jemima shook her head, a clear sign of dismissal. "That's all well and good for you. However, I've been doing this for longer than you have, and I've been drinking tea for longer than you have. Not to mention, I am much less klutzy. So," she said as if she'd made her point, "I will be served breakfast in the archives. By you."

Anna had no choice but to agree. And as she left the house, all she got from Rose was a smile and a simple nod. "I'll see you tomorrow morning, Anna, hmm?"

But like the trained, polite gal she was, she nodded. "Yes, Mrs. Horowitz-Margareten, you will."

THE MEETING WITH JIDS brass went well. They'd answered his questions and gave him enough information to prepare his agenda for the meeting with Evan Lefkowitz the next day.

He hoped it was enough to convince Evan to sponsor the new JIDS policy arm.

But there was something else he had to take care of, something important. Jacob had sent out a bunch of emails to various museums and private collections, and he needed to see if they'd gotten back to him.

One of them had. He opened the email and read:

Jemima Kellerman started her career with us. It ended unceremoniously when important papers went missing from the Kuflik collection and she'd been the

intern working with them. If you have any questions, feel free to follow up.

And there it was, in plain, clear language.

His mother had been right; there was, in fact, a difference between having suspicions, hearing words spoken in conversations in a whisper network, and having concrete evidence. Gathering that evidence gave him a purpose.

Gave him something to focus on that wasn't just the mistake he'd made.

And the heart he'd broken.

He went through the notes, checked the time, and called Tony's cell.

The phone rang a few times, which made Jacob stare at the clock, hoping he'd gotten the time correct. Finally, an answer. "Tony Liu, this is after office hours. Did you see that the Empires drafted Ben Klein?"

"I hadn't," he said. "First round. Good choice. Listen, I have a few ridiculous thoughts for you about the Mitzvah Alliance projects back in the manor."

"I love it when you have ridiculous thoughts. Tell me."

He talked about the policy arm and the search for an educator for public policy. He talked about his ideas and his dreams.

"That's great," Tony said. "I'll put the money together, prepare for a donation for the salary for the educator. But that's not the only reason why you're calling me now. What's going on?"

Jacob took a breath. "Look in on Anna for me. I can't be back until at least tomorrow night, but I figured as long as I was going to ask you about this—"

"—you could also ask me or Charlotte to check in on Anna."

"Don't let her know. I don't want to worry her."

"You're on speaker. So why didn't you ask her yourself?"

He pulled himself together and poured his heart out to his friend, and his wife. "So yeah. The last person in the world she wants to hear from is me. But I'm worried."

"I can't believe you, Jacob," Charlotte said in the background. "But if she needs a friend, she'll have one."

"And," Tony added, "I'll keep you posted on the other. I'll email you later tonight."

"Thank you," Jacob said. "I owe you more than I can say."

Chapter Eighteen

ANNA WAS VERY lucky. Dinner with her grandmother that night was wonderful, and the chocolate chip cookies Charlotte had delivered hit the right spot. It felt good. Almost good enough to make her forget the errands she had to manage.

She got to Charlotte's bakery early the next morning, chatted with her friend, and ordered Jemima's tea to go.

"You're going to be fine," Charlotte said. "No matter what. I'll be here. Text me if you need me, okay?"

But as Anna left the shop, the tea cup in a holder, the perfect, flaky croissant in a bag, a sense of foreboding bubbled up in her stomach, practically erupting as she drove up the long driveway to the back entrance of Rockliffe, the one closest to the archives. She didn't want to walk inside. She reached into her bag, making sure she had her box of gloves as she normally did when she headed into the archives. Even if Jemima wasn't going to follow the rules about document handling, she certainly was.

As she headed to the door, she realized she needed to disarm the security system. Except it seemed someone already had.

"Hello?" she called.

"Oh, come right in, Anna," Jemima said, waving her hand, smiling. "Bring the tea right over, will you?"

Anna tried not to look completely horrified at the vision she came across when she stepped into the archives. Jemima was sitting at the table, gorgeous photographs of Horowitz-Margareten ancestors in ball gowns arrayed around her. Gloves were nowhere to be found. "I…"

"Oh pish. Aren't these spectacular? They're just the thing I want for my exhibit. And you'll write beautiful cards for them, okay?"

What could she say but "yes"?

"Oh come on, Anna. Give me the tea, and we can chat more about your little project in ways where we can make sure we're focusing on the grandeur of these people, this family."

"Are you sure?" Anna held out the cup and the bag.

Jemima took both the cup and the bag. "Oh for God's sake, Anna."

Jemima sat and placed the bag in front of her. As Anna put on the gloves appropriate for handling photographs, Jemima pursed her lips in distaste and gestured widely, swiping at the cup with her elbow, knocking the tea all over the photographs.

Anna watched the droplets of tea fall to the ground; the damage they caused to priceless artifacts was incalculable.

She couldn't move.

The door creaked open, the squeaking hinges breaking through the silence, and Anna's heart practically broke through her chest.

JACOB WOKE UP to three different emails and two voicemails. One of the emails confirmed his meeting in a few hours with Tikkun Online founder Evan Lefkowitz. The second message was a blistering voicemail from Charlotte, who let him know Anna's mask of joy was not fooling anybody and that he was lucky she was still talking to him.

But the most important message was the voicemail he'd received from the director of the California Museum of the Jewish People.

Hi, Jacob. I wanted to let you know Jemima Kellerman caused significant damage to the Krupp family collection. Photographs and priceless documents were stained and then removed from the collection because of her careless actions. She was let go soon after the damage was discovered. I've sent you appropriate, not private of course, documentation that was placed in her file. Let me know if you need anything further.

—Alice Wagner

That upped the number of records he now had to five,

including in that bunch the communication he'd gotten the day before from the Kuflik collection. Five very similar, documented cases of damage and theft from collections across the country. He asked his assistant to print the emails and bind them along with the supplementary documentation so that he could take them back to New York.

All he had to do was get through one more meeting in Austin. Once that was over, he could go back to Rockliffe with the documents or bring them wherever else they needed to go.

And for once in his life, it seemed like one was way too many.

⇢⟫⟩⟨⟨⟨⇠

ANNA COULDN'T CONSIDER anything as vital as breathing.

The archives were painfully silent, Rose staring at the two of them as if she was about to explode, her cheeks getting redder and redder, her hands fisting and unfisting and ending in the pockets of her pants. Her eyes were narrow slits.

"What. The. Hell. Happened. Here?"

Her words were punctuated, as if she'd spit them out of her mouth one by one.

"My assistant," Jemima began, her voice edging into pouting territory, "was careless with my instructions and has caused incalculable damage."

"The instructions," Anna interjected despite everything screaming inside of her to stop, "I didn't want to follow because I told you it would be a mistake. I didn't want to bring you tea and a croissant into the archives, but you insisted."

"It doesn't matter who followed whose advice," Rose began, glaring at them both. "The protocols are that no food or drink was to be consumed in this area, and let's not even get into the conversation about how gloves were to be worn when handling photographs especially."

"You know," Jemima interjected, "it is quite controversial in the community about the wearing of gloves. Anna herself could tell you that one shouldn't wear gloves while handling photographs."

Anna sighed, reached into her bag, and pulled out her gloves. "I've been wearing these all week, and if I were to actually touch the photographs, I'd wear them. I follow the rules of the site I'm researching on."

Rose glared at her. "As if one measly pair of gloves will nullify the damage done by both food and drink in this area. I thought better of you, Anna. Much better."

Anna tried to keep her temper as Jemima dismissed her with a wave. "My assistant really messed up in this area, and it is entirely my fault for even suggesting she involve herself in this project with me. It is entirely my responsibility for even thinking it would be a good idea to send an assistant curator to do a curator's job, and you have my apologies."

"Miss Kellerman," Rose began, and even as scared as she was, Anna could hear steel in the older woman's voice. "You—"

"No," Jemima interrupted in a way only fools spoke to someone like Rose. "My assistant was responsible for handling the documents; my assistant was responsible for the faulty procedures she followed. She should take all of the blame and all of the consequences."

Anna needed to make her position clear. "I've been working here for a month. Following protocols you established. Working long hours and organizing the archives. I loved doing this, because the project is important. But let me make this clear: once the rules changed, once things weren't my responsibility, this was what happened. Say what you will, but don't blame this on me."

For a moment, Anna thought she saw understanding in Rose's eyes. "Very well, I won't. The fact of the matter is, both of you are responsible. Both of you, please leave the archives. Immediately."

The verdict had been delivered.

Anna had made her stand; she'd done her best. And she was okay with the consequences. Because she had work to do for the Historical Society, and possibly the Jewish Center.

But just the same, she walked with Jemima out of the building.

"You should consider yourself terminated from your employment," Jemima said. "No reasonable person would hire you after this."

"Good luck getting to the train station," she replied as she headed to her car, determined to plot out her next move.

>>>>——<<<<

JACOB WAS PACING in Evan Lefkowitz's office. They were supposed to be having a meeting, but all he could focus on was the series of increasingly frantic emails that an increasing number of people from Rockliffe Manor were sending him, following the texts that had clogged his phone earlier.

"Give me a second?"

Lefkowitz nodded. "By all means."

He got back into his email and saw that Jemima had caused damage to some of the archival photographs. A quick check into one of the few databases that his relatives had created showed him that at least one of them was also in the Jewish Center's collection. He took a breath.

"I have to make a phone call," he said as he headed out of the office. "You don't have to worry about the photographs," he said, not even waiting for his mother to say more than a hello. "I've got to finish this meeting and then I'll head to the Jewish Center before…"

"Do you have the information?" his mother interjected. "Because that's what we need right now. Not just the photographs."

"I do. I'll get it before I head back."

"And you know that I had to banish both of them from the archives? Jemima took that out on Anna."

He blew out a breath.

"I'm on my way," he said. "We'll decide if it's better for me to go to the city or the Jewish Center on the way back."

He walked back into the office, and Evan Lefkowitz was looking through pages on his desk.

His timing, this time, had been the worst.

Jacob grabbed the arm of his chair, and he forced himself to breathe. Tried to desperately remind himself that the worst thing he could do at this moment was to run out of this man's office and get on a plane.

There were people who needed him to make this connection.

"Everything okay?"

"Things at home are a bit of a mess," he said. "A few fires I need to put out."

The other man nodded, slowly. "I get it," he said. "Family is important. We can do this later. You're not far from Jersey."

"I'm mostly on Long Island these days, so yes."

"Well then. We can talk about immigration reform and a policy arm for JIDS at a Pixies game...unless you're a Mermaids fan?"

Interesting. Hockey.

He'd been a fan of the Legends when they started because they were a sister team to the Empires, but maybe

Anna would want to bring a bunch of her friends to a Mermaids game on the Island. "I'm actually a Legends fan," he replied. "But I would like to get to know the game a bit better, see it through the perspective of someone who has first-hand knowledge of how it works."

And just like that, the meeting was over, with every single sign that Evan Lefkowitz was going to sponsor the policy arm.

More importantly, Jacob had admitted that he wasn't perfect, and instead of closing the door, Evan Lefkowitz had walked right through it, offering both understanding and support, demonstrating he was someone Jacob could work with in the future.

Maybe Jacob could trust people.

All he knew was that he had to get back to Rockliffe Manor and fix the problems Jemima had created. And maybe, hopefully, some of the ones he had as well.

BEFORE SHE PULLED out of the Rockliffe drive, Anna sent emails to Charlotte, Dr. Humphries, and her grandmother; emails to both her grandmother and Rivvy asked them to contact Rabbi Davidson.

Love. Friendship. A situation she was going to fix herself, and a career she was going to build on her own from the ashes of the old. At least for now.

But when she stepped past the threshold, Rivvy, Charlotte, and Oma embraced her; amazing smells of bagels, cream cheese, and lox filled the air.

"Dr. Humphries is on her way," Oma said once Anna had stepped out of the embrace and blown her nose. "She's going to join us here."

"Rabbi Davidson's on her way, too," Rivvy said. "I also think the rabbi and Dr. Humphries might have a plan for you."

"But…"

"You're under contract to the Historical Society," Dr. Humphries said as she stepped through the hallway and entered the room. "The subsidy was provided mostly by a grant the Horowitz-Margareten family made to the society, but the contract is not with the foundation. You're working for me, my dear, and I always will have use for someone with your skills."

"And," the rabbi added as she joined the group, "it was great to see you the last time you joined the Jewish Center research circle, and I strongly suspect that the group preparing the Jewish Center's booth for Summer Days would have need of your expertise. In exchange, the board of the Jewish Center would love to contribute part of the stipend in exchange for some future archival work."

Then the rabbi and Dr. Humphries exchanged glances with her grandmother, and after a while, the rabbi stepped forward to speak. "When can you start?"

Soon after, the rabbi drove Anna to the Jewish Center and installed her in the library, with guidance from Rivvy's notes. She had her hair back, gloves and mask on, careful to not destroy the photographs she was looking through. The congregation had a fascinating history, and diving into that was a balm to her soul.

"Break time."

Rivvy smiled and entered the room. "Come on, it's after two thirty, and I'm hungry. Charlotte is outside with food."

Anna smiled. She followed Rivvy into the courtyard and realized how lucky she was. "Thank you," she said.

"It's important," Charlotte said as she joined her friend, "that we stick together no matter what happens."

Rivvy smiled. "Yep. We're friends regardless."

She was lucky. So lucky. She had landed on her feet. And she was loved.

Chapter Nineteen

T HE NEXT MORNING, Anna started work at the Historical Society, and halfway through, she received an email from, of all people, Rose.

Dear Anna,

I am most likely the last person you would like to see right now, but as a gesture of apology, I would like to invite you to lunch at Goldberg's. I have things I must explain to you, and though I know you don't have to, I would very much like you to hear them out.

Humbly,
Rose Horowitz-Margareten

Professionally, Anna still was interested in a career in curation, and a reference from Rose would be invaluable. Personally, Rose was one of Oma's closest friends, and leaving a rift would hurt her grandmother.

And Jacob. No matter where they stood.

Prepared, she cracked her knuckles and she emailed Rose back.

Dear Mrs. Horowitz-Margareten,

What time?

Anna

Which meant when her watch went off at one o'clock, she said goodbye to Beatrice and headed over to Goldberg's. The inside of that restaurant had seen so much of her life in Rockliffe Manor, it was only fitting that she have this conversation here, too.

"Ah," the older woman said, "you're here." Rose beamed and waved to the maître d', who smiled back at her. His vest was pressed and his tie was a perfect bow.

He waved back and simply pointed.

"This place," Rose gestured widely, "and your grandmother were both very, very helpful in ways that neither of them would suspect nor acknowledge. In the manner of surviving my marriage, of course."

Anna decided that it was probably better for her to eat the kasha varnishkes and derma on the menu than contemplate how unprepared she was to handle a conversation that started that way. "I'm not sure why I'm here," Anna said instead of confronting a few of those unexpected feelings. "But you said you had things to tell me?"

Rose took a sip of her seltzer. "Yes," she said. "I have both personal and professional things I should tell you. They are intertwined in a way, and both are important."

Instead of answering, Anna grabbed a kreplach and started to chew on it.

"In a few days you'll find out that Jemima Kellerman is

no longer the curator at the Manhattan Museum of Jewish History."

If that weren't an opening salvo, she wasn't sure what was. "I don't know what to say to that? How is that possible?"

"A few things happened behind the scenes. She has a record of causing damage in private collections, and documentations of the instances where she had done so were compiled, the appropriate people gathered as witnesses. Along with our statement and the record of the photographs that had been on loan to the Jewish Center, the case against Jemima was proven beyond a reasonable doubt if not in a court of law." Rose smiled again. "In light of all of that evidence, the museum had no choice but to act. And quickly."

"But what does that mean to me? I still have no job, and it seems I was used as bait."

Rose shook her head. "No. Definitely not bait. There were multiple factors at play two days ago, and you, the person we were most trying to protect, ended up caught in the crossfire. The situation should have been planned better and handled with more care. You should have been handled with care. You didn't deserve what happened, and I'm truly sorry. I don't deserve your forgiveness, but I do apologize for my failures and my part in hurting you."

"Multiple factors?" she managed. "What do you mean?"

Rose sighed. "This goes into the personal situation, why I

say they were intertwined. Jacob never trusted your boss. He trusted you, but not her. And the problem was, you were working for someone; I had to give her access, and he made it very clear that I wasn't to interfere in your career."

"I'm still confused," Anna said.

"I understand. There is a great deal of information, but all of that leads to the fact that my hands were tied. Except when I told Jacob that your job was in danger, he acted, pulling together the evidence and organizing the witnesses. Every single one of them. Then he came back to New York to deliver them personally to the museum."

She'd told him to leave.

He'd come to her aid even when they weren't on speaking terms.

This was a lot.

"There are other things I need to tell you about my son, I think." Rose sighed again. "This is when I start to get personal, and where I require your indulgence. As children, you and Jacob built a bond that was stronger than anybody anticipated, and the name, the legacy, everything, would have crushed you both had I not intervened. Or at least that's what I thought."

"What do you mean?"

"I didn't know what was best for Jacob. He was a very serious child, and there was so much to teach him. I didn't want him to have the same relationship to money and position as his father did. And so that was my primary focus.

I'm worried that I overcompensated, ended up shorting him on the kinds of things that would help him in a relationship. Because he only feels he's enough if he's perfect. He feels as if he is only useful if he's doing things for others, and he doesn't let anybody in."

Anna shook her head. "We don't know. Life is uncertain. Maybe your meddling saved him from being someone like his father. I don't know. But part of growing up is learning what's important and fixing things that need fixing."

"Which is very kind of you to say, but what *I* am saying is that if I had the chance to do it over again, I would have guided him in a way that would have supported a relationship instead of leading to separation."

"Okay," Anna said as she took another kreplach. "I appreciate the apology and adore you for wanting to help, but in the end this is truly about Jacob and I, not anybody else. We love our families. I mean, I love mine and I know he loves you, but we are still individuals and need to figure out things for ourselves. Our history will always be a part of us, but we have to make our own future."

"How did someone so young become so wise?" Rose replied, shaking her head. "I think you're right. I just want so much for you both to be happy." She paused. "I will suggest, however, that you think about what you want to do professionally, regardless of what you want to do personally. When you hear about the open position, you will receive a letter from the museum director, asking for a plan. Think about one and put it together. You have my support and anything you might need to make that happen."

"Thank you," she said. "I appreciate that."

"It is," Rose said, taking a kreplach of her own, "the very least I can do."

And as their lunch arrived, Anna started to think about her future, both who and what she wanted in it.

JACOB SETTLED INTO the chair in his Manhattan office. He was only minutes away from the most important meeting of his lifetime.

Totally nothing to make a big deal about.

He blew out a breath, checked his email and his phone.

Finally, there was a knock at the door. "Come in," he said.

Anna's mother walked in, not pausing for formalities, just moved to sit at the chair in front of his desk. "I have to tell you that I didn't expect to hear from you. I was intrigued by your email."

"Intrigued is good," he replied. "Intrigued is very good because I'm trying to help Mitzvah Alliance sponsor as well as create a framework for the Jewish Immigrant Defense Society's potential policy arm."

"You're working with Mitzvah Alliance?"

He wasn't exactly going to tell her that he'd founded

Mitzvah Alliance just yet, so he hedged a little. "Behind the scenes. Anyway, JIDS wants a policy arm, so we're trying to build it for them."

Anna's mother settled down into the seat across from his desk. "I am definitely intrigued. But tell me, Jacob. Why me? Why now?"

He shrugged. "Look. I wouldn't be lying if I pointed out how convenient this was, that of the top-ten experts teaching public policy at universities in the United States, one of them is the mother of the woman I…love."

Dr. Green-Cohen nodded. "Yes. That is convenient. Extremely so. And I find the work that the Mitzvah Alliance has been doing fascinating for an organization so new. It's obvious the organization is driven to do something bigger in this world. Better."

"You asked me what I do that makes me an ethical billionaire," he replied, "and a large part of that is the work I do through Mitzvah Alliance, the things I do to make the world better."

"I think there's something huge missing here," Anna's mother replied. "And if you don't mind, I need to give you some advice?"

He nodded. "I can listen to advice."

"One of the most important things in this world, aside from love, aside from doing your best, is knowing what makes you happy." She paused, and he met her eyes with his own. "There were many reasons Anna spent childhood summers with my parents—my work was one of them, wanting her to be close with my parents was another. But the unexpected byproduct was that it allowed my husband and I to do the things that permitted us to be fully engaged with family during the year. I could go to practices, I could help with homework because I'd finished so much of the groundwork for the year over the summers. And my husband, my dear supportive husband, and I spent time together. We remembered our happy places and found them. You are driven, very much so, as is Anna. And those are very good things. But it is vitally important for any healthy relationship to be able to find those happy places, to bask in those moments. Together."

He nodded. "For the record," he said, "I don't know what's going to happen with Anna and I. I have my hopes, of course. We have our own present to grapple with, but I appreciate the insight."

Anna's mother nodded. "Fair enough, and I do understand. Now, of course, I think we have things to talk about."

As they talked about the program and what the commitment would be like, Jacob started to think about his own future.

And his happiness.

Chapter Twenty

AFTER A LONG, wild night and a day that made little sense, Anna left the Historical Society and headed to the train station to pick up Batya.

"I don't know why you're doing this," her friend said. "There are taxis and hired cars and other ways I can use to get from the train station to your grandmother's house by myself."

"Yeah, but I haven't seen you in a while; things are a bit wild here."

Batya raised an eyebrow. "Wild? Better or worse since the video chat?"

On the drive, Anna told Batya the whole story, from the beginning. Including the part where she'd lost her job, the conversation she'd had with Rose the day before, and the situation she now found herself in.

"That is," Batya said after thinking a minute and adjusting her glasses, "interesting to say the least. Wow. Have you made any decisions about any of this?"

Anna shook her head. "Not really. Not yet."

"Think away, my friend." Batya paused as they entered

the house and collapsed on the couch. "But for now," she asked as she gestured toward the television, "how do you feel about watching Sam Moskowitz and his *tuchus* for a few hours?"

Anna grinned. "That sounds perfect," she said as she searched for and found the most recent *Shadow Squad* movie on her streaming service and pressed play.

A few hours later, after a wonderful dinner with her grandmother and Batya, Anna sat at the kitchen table with a cup of tea and thinking.

Batya poured water into her teacup. "What's up? What am I in for tomorrow?"

Anna shrugged. "You're going to meet my friend Rivvy at town hall in the morning, and I've got stuff to do at the Jewish Center."

"Any ideas about what you want?"

Anna sighed. "Now that's the big question, right?"

Batya took a sip from her teacup and sighed. "What are you leaning toward?"

"Don't know. It feels like there's a lot of things I want, and I'm not sure if I can have them all."

Batya stood and crossed the table to sit down next to her. "So, have you made a list?"

Anna shook her head. "No. I haven't. Not yet."

"You should," Batya said as she took a sip of her tea. "Write it all down. Make what you want into words as opposed to nebulous ideas. That will give you specific...not goals, per se, but objectives."

"I'm so good at seeing big picture, organizing a story out of a collection of facts and making an exhibit come to life. But when it comes to this, I can't decide what I really want."

"You can organize everybody else. Not yourself. And you need to organize yourself. You know what? Here." Batya shoved a pen and a piece of paper into her hand. "This is how you do that."

Anna thought about it before taking the pen and writing down a bunch of things. Archives. Exhibits at the museum.

But it was way too overwhelming to even think about. She dropped the pen and shook her head. "It's impossible. It's too much. Way too much."

Batya laughed. "I think you need to figure out which one is most important and go from there. You know Sarah works for both the bookstore and the library, right?"

"Yes," Anna said as the ideas started to flow. "She does events for both. I wonder if it's possible to work both with the museum and a few other places, doing special exhibits?"

"Good. Now you're thinking. What about relationships?"

She sighed. "Jacob is still…confusing. But he stepped in behind the scenes to make sure I was professionally vindicated. I don't know what to do with that."

"Well," Batya said, "maybe you need to think about why he did that. And what that means. You could also just ask him."

Anna nodded. "I could. Maybe…see what he's been up to?"

"You could." Batya nodded. "You definitely could. Because as I recall, this is up to you."

Jacob had walked away, she remembered. She couldn't get the way he'd turned his back on her out of her head.

Except there was one clear omission she'd made: he'd only walked away because she told him to. Jacob was many things, but he was especially good at observing boundaries she'd set. He was also a good listener.

Which meant he'd never approach her without her opening the door first.

"It is up to me," she said aloud.

"So what are you going to do about it?"

Having made her decision, Anna reached for her phone and sent Jacob a text.

⫸⫷

JACOB ALMOST DROPPED the phone into his water glass.

He didn't know what Anna wanted, why she had texted, but he definitely was going to take her up on whatever it was. And so he arranged to meet her at the library at about noon.

Neutral territory. Safe ground. History. Their history. Rockliffe Manor's history.

His thoughts, words, everything but the sight of her evaporated as she came down the stairs of the library. She'd always stolen his breath, but here, now, he savored her image as if it was the last time he was going to see her.

"Hi," he said.

She looked away; there was something just below the surface of her gaze and he couldn't figure it out. "So, I wanted to thank you."

"For?"

"Intervening, you know, with Jemima."

He shook his head. "That was all her. All I did was point out that this wasn't the first time she'd damaged priceless family relics in private archives. Eminently believable, remember?"

Which was probably not the best reference to make, bringing them back to the conversation where he'd told her the reason he'd ignored her in December. But that was all he had, that was the way he saw things.

There was a pause before she spoke, like she wasn't sure how to handle the situation. As if he'd surprised her. "So, it wasn't me you stepped in for?"

Bad surprise.

Right.

He had to get this right. Because he hadn't stepped in for her; he hated the idea of intervening in her career even when they were on better terms. But this? This wasn't a normal situation, and he had to make his feelings clear. Lead with his emotions and not completely fumble this. "I told you I trust you," he replied. "Even back at the bar, I told you I trusted you. I believe in you, Anna."

Which was closer to dealing with his emotions than he'd been since he'd left her. "Anyway," he said into the silence, "I knew it was her because I didn't trust her. You'd never treat things so callously."

She raised an eyebrow. "Things?"

"Yeah. Documents, photographs, anything." He shoved his hands into his pockets, looked away from her. This was like fighting against gravity. "Anyway, I hope you get everything you want. You deserve the world on a platter, and I'm…I didn't."

He caught a glimpse of a smile. Where had that come from?

"I didn't realize you were Atlas, you know."

He laughed. Because that's all he could do. "No. I'm not. You deserved better from me. Always."

"I deserve *you*." Her words were slow, as if she were creating them out of nothing. Was this as hard for her as it was for him?

He didn't say anything. What could he say?

"For better or worse, you know?"

He didn't. Not at all. "I don't…"

She ran a hand through her hair; it was a tell. He could see the nerves there.

"*I* don't want an outline of where you are," she said, her words hesitant as she met his eyes. "If we're doing this, for real, no backward or sideways or halfsies or whatever, I want *you.* Warts and all."

Wait.

His heart stopped. Cold.

Had she? Was she asking him if he wanted to try again? To start over once again? For *real?* To give their relationship yet another chance?

He didn't want to ask, but he had to clarify for his own sake and the blood pounding in his ears. "Are you saying...what I think you're saying?"

She smiled. "If you're up for it, if you'll let me in, for real this time, I'm asking you if you want to give this another try?"

"Yes." He couldn't have said yes fast enough, so he said it again. "Yes."

"Sealed with a kiss?"

"I thought you'd never ask," he said as he leaned closer, placed his lips on hers and lost himself in the taste of her, in the kiss, in the way her skin felt under his fingertips. The way her scent intoxicated him.

He didn't want to move, but when she broke the kiss, her eyes were as bright as the brightest stars.

KISSING JACOB WAS so all-consuming that Anna had managed to forget where she was.

In the middle of Rockliffe Manor, *downtown Rockliffe*

Manor.

Which was probably not the best of ideas, so she broke the kiss, leaving Jacob looking as if he'd woken up from a dream.

"So," she said, making good on her promises to herself, and starting on the right foot this time, "maybe you can take me around the village, show me what you've been up to here?"

He raised an eyebrow, and she could see the hesitancy in his eyes. That was absolutely her fault. "You mean the BID and the plans."

She nodded. She had no idea where the Business Improvement District he was talking about was, but she wanted to see it. "All of it. Would that work?"

"Yes." He nodded.

But what did it for her, what sealed that deal was the look in his eyes: of joy, of pride and of excitement. And that warmed her all the way down to her toes. "I'll take you everywhere."

Everywhere.

She couldn't respond fast enough; the words that would explain how she'd follow him to the ends of the earth got caught in her mouth, her excitement tied in her tongue.

As the silence built between them, the noises she managed instead of words made him fluster, pull back.

"Um…in town?"

"Everywhere," she replied, as if the vacuum seal had broken. "I mean you don't only work in Rockliffe Manor. You do things in the city and you work with organizations in Texas. I want to know about all of them. All of this…"

He blinked. "What? You mean in Texas?

"Yeah," she said. Wow. His surprise was absolutely her fault. "I want you to tell me about that, how it started and everything else."

She'd never asked him about the things he was doing; she'd been supportive, proud of him for doing things when they were together, but she'd never actually asked him about any of them. And the effects of that were obvious and made her feel positively awful.

"Okay. Absolutely." Then he smiled, pulled his phone out of his pocket.

"What's up?"

"One quick thing, and let's do this."

She nodded, waited. Hoped for the best. What could he be doing? What could he be asking for?

Finally he turned, and looked up at her. The light in his eyes was so beautiful, the smile he gave her was so free, she could tell whatever he'd arranged on the phone was for her.

"*Now* let's do this."

And there was nothing else she wanted to do. Nothing in the world.

"It started," he began as if he was guiding her like a typical tourist, "just beyond the border of the house, near the water. Now it's grown"—he waved a hand, gesturing at the enlarged business district. "And we've got plans to let it keep growing in ways that work with the town."

She smiled. "Work with the town, huh?"

"Exactly. We don't want development that steps on the town footprint. We want to reuse buildings and make new businesses out of the old. So we're paying attention to housing needs and food needs and—"

She took his hand, and his fingers felt marvelous. "I'm ready," she said. "Show me."

And she listened as he told her about how the post office building was a repurposed factory and the brand-new daycare center was reclaimed office space.

He explained that office space in the community center was rent-free for those who needed it, as long as the organization participated in festivals like Summer Days that brought Rockliffe Manor's population together. The Chinese Society, the local branch of the NAACP, and a few other groups shared space, and Wednesday night cookouts, with the rest of the town.

And when he took her through the back entrance at Charlotte's bakery, she started to laugh.

The electric candles and the instructions were clear; the sweet lemonade, jam, gloves and folding instructions were clearer.

"You are ridiculous," she said, grinning at him as she tried to fold along the lines.

"Do you want to do it together?" he asked.

Of course she did. She wanted to fold dough, to make hamantaschen with him. "I'd love to."

He stepped behind her, and she covered his hands with her own.

"Like this," he whispered, gently folding the edges, her fingers following his patterns.

And a few hours later Charlotte and Tony had arrived to see them both covered in flour and sugar.

"Oh my God, you two. Can you just not be so adorable?"

She laughed; they'd never been called adorable by anybody, but as Charlotte was letting them use her oven and the back of her bakery, it was more than okay.

"These are so good," Anna managed after Charlotte had pulled them out of the oven, flour most likely still on her nose.

"What are they again?" Tony asked.

"Hamantaschen," Jacob explained. "They're a traditional treat for the Jewish holiday of Purim. Harder pastry on the outside, jam on the inside."

And as the four of them continued to chat and enjoy dessert, she realized why it was so appropriate that they'd baked hamantaschen together.

Because, quite simply, to her, Jacob was a hamantaschen, the hard shell outside with the visible soft center for anybody who really and truly saw him. Sarah, she thought, could have her ruggelach. She preferred her hamantaschen any day of the week.

Chapter Twenty-One

THE NEXT DAY, Anna was finishing up the research for the Jewish Center's exhibit, and was just about to go and join Rivvy and Batya at the setup near the outdoor café when she saw Jacob leaning against the doorframe of the Jewish Center's library.

"Well, hello there," she said. "Nice to see you."

"Thought I'd stop by," he said, "you know, see how you were doing?"

She smiled. This felt *good*. "It's going. But I was just about to finish up."

"Do you want dinner?"

She paused for a second, thought about it. "Yes," she replied. "I'd love to have dinner with you."

"Really?"

"Yes," she said, enjoying the way his eyes brightened and his smile widened at the thought. "You have perfect timing."

"Is that the only thing you like of mine?"

She laughed. "Quit while you're ahead. Let me finish up and we can go."

"So my timing was that perfect, huh?" he asked later

when they were sitting at a Thai restaurant. "I mean, I didn't have to say much."

She smiled as she looked up at him. "My stomach had informed me that it needed to take center stage."

"Reasonable," he replied. "Have you decided what you want?"

"Pad Se-Ew with chicken," she said. "Nothing else at this point."

He took a swallow of his iced tea. "Okay. What's stopping you?"

"I can't help thinking that there are tons of different special collections I'd love to work with, as well as working in conjunction with the museum."

"So you want that freedom, hmm?"

"I do," she replied as she let the ideas flow. "Like, say if the Grove Hotel offered me the opportunity to create an exhibit of the dreidels they've commissioned over the years, or if a museum somewhere wanted to partner to do an exhibit on the history of Jewish social justice in their area, you know?"

He tapped his fingers on the table. "I like that idea, a lot. I can also see you partnering with say, someone like Penina Alton-Schrader or Melanie Gould and creating exhibits in conjunction with their books, maybe as some kind of launch party for them? Which means you'd need a deal with the museum that would permit you that freedom."

Which was the dream job she'd written down when she

was with Batya. But Jacob was someone who'd recently interacted in some capacity with the people who'd be receiving this proposal, which meant he might have some kind of understanding of how they'd react to it. "Do you think they'd go for it? I was an assistant curator."

"Who was wrongfully terminated, and who has a gift at telling stories through documents and bringing history to life on the walls."

"Speaking of which," she said, carefully. "We haven't really talked about the whole"—she sighed—"the whole situation. With the archives."

He took another drink of tea. "We haven't, and we should. I told you I would point out every person I'd be dealing with that I don't want you near, and I think when your work comes up against…involves my family, we should talk about it. At any level. My feelings, whether there are people and family histories that we don't want public, and then we decide between ourselves, together, how it's going to go. You're the archivist, which is true, but you're also…well, you're also family. And you deserve the full story. Warts and all."

"That makes sense," she replied, especially the part where he said she was family too. "And because we'll be talking about what we're doing, when and where, and our schedules, it won't be that difficult to suss out these kinds of situations." She paused "You know, when I have a situation to talk about."

"I'm convinced you will," he replied, his gaze intense. "I say you should ask for what you want. All of it. Reach for the stars, Anna. You have galaxies to build."

As she enjoyed the dinner, and the kisses that tasted like the ice cream Jacob insisted they needed, followed by the drive back to her grandmother's house, she realized she had to figure out what she was reaching for.

Because the truth was that she already knew who she was reaching with.

Chapter Twenty-Two

AFTER JACOB AND his very welcome coffee delivery left the Jewish Center the next morning, Anna focused on finishing the packing process. She started to box up the smaller items, like the photo albums and the notes that were going to be taped to the table, as well as the bundles of brochures printed for this specific purpose. The RMJC had a wonderful history and she was excited on this gorgeous day to help the town learn more about it.

Which made her pause and pick up her phone. The text from the head of the museum had been sitting, unanswered in her inbox since the late hours of last night.

Hope all is well with you. I am searching for ideas on how to make the position you wish for. You have been an asset to both the museum and the Rockliffe project, and we would very much like to have your input.

I will be in Rockliffe Manor for the next few days attending the festival as a guest of the Horowitz-Margareten family and look forward to meeting you, along with the head of the Horowitz-Margareten Foundation.

Ideas danced in Anna's head. But more prominently was what Batya had told her about Sarah's position, and Jacob's excitement about the idea of her doing special collection work as well as working at the museum.

Could she have it all? Could she have the kind of position she wanted?

She could, only if she asked for it.

Reach for the stars, Jacob had said. *You have galaxies to build.*

Once she'd finished boxing up the last of the items, she said a quick goodbye to the rabbi and the members of the committee who were still at the Jewish Center and drove to her grandmother's house.

"I've got a plan," she told her grandmother as she walked in.

"Good," Oma said, smiling. "I'm glad to hear it."

And then, she dashed off two emails.

To whom it may concern,

I would like to convene a meeting with all parties to this discussion at 1 p.m. Please let me know if this is possible and what location.

Respectfully,
Anna Cohen

And after she hit send on the first one, she sent a second.

Jacob,

I really hope you'll be there.

Yours,
Anna

Both the museum director and Rose, as the head of the foundation, quickly agreed to meet her at the foundation offices.

But her heart pounded as she stared at her inbox, waiting for Jacob's response.

Finally, her phone vibrated, and as she clicked on the message, she saw it was from Jacob. She held her breath, and opened the message:

Anna,

Wouldn't miss it for the world.

Yours, Jacob

Relief filled her body from head to toe, and she let herself relax in the moment.

He was coming.

Then she plugged in her phone, and headed off to make herself presentable. She was going to do this.

JACOB'S HEART HAD been pounding since he responded to Anna's email. He finished up what he'd been doing at the Historical Society, then headed over to the foundation offices.

He wasn't the first to arrive though; his mother and the museum director were already there. He checked his watch: still early.

But they seemed impatient, tapping the table as they sat in conversation about trivialities.

"Have you seen her?" his mother asked.

"She'll be here," he said, with a shrug. "She doesn't ever set deadlines she doesn't meet."

The doors blew open, and Anna walked in. He couldn't help but stare at her. He always found her beautiful, but at this moment? She was powerful. This was someone who'd found inner strength, decided what she wanted, and was going for it. And he couldn't love her more, not in that moment or ever.

"All of you are wondering what I'm looking for, and I have ideas."

He couldn't help the huge sigh of relief he let out, though seeing her expression made him wish he had.

And as she outlined her plan—working for the museum and the foundation, organizing its archives—his heart burst with pride. She was taking what she wanted.

But would she reach for the stars?

"My favorite part of all of this," Anna continued, "is that I'd very much like the chance to create exhibits and special projects that mean something to me at the museum *and* outside of it, with the help of a new curator, one who would be interested in not just making assistants do the grunt work but also taking the time to teach and mentor new assistants."

He took a few notes, before looking back up at her. He loved her. He loved this proposal. So much. And yet, the surprise on the museum director's face was something he hadn't considered.

Had the director thought Anna would suggest herself for the head curator's position?

"Not just me, of course," Anna continued as if she were clarifying. "There are so many assistant curators who deserve exhibits of their own, and so many more who should be joining the staff. The museum needs to be a vibrant place that tells *all* Jewish history. We are a beautiful, diverse population with a history that needs to be celebrated. *All of us.*"

The museum director and his mother both nodded. And he couldn't help smiling. "You've given us a lot to think about," the director said. "We'll talk in a few days, hmm?"

"At the Ball," his mother said.

Which was in a few days. Too long for his own purposes, but he could see the validity in the timeframe.

So he took his cue from Anna. "Sounds good to me," she said. "Thank you for listening."

"Oh and Anna," his mother interjected, "I know you must have a bunch of things to handle this afternoon, but do you think you can come over to the house later?"

"Later?" Anna asked. "Not till about five, I don't think. I have to take care of details for both the Historical Society and the Jewish Center, and it's going to take a while."

"Five is fine," his mother replied.

Anna smiled, and at last, the meeting was done. So many

questions still to be answered. So much to discuss. He couldn't wait.

ANNA FELT WARM and fuzzy in a very particular way as she left the meeting.

And it all had to do with Jacob.

Having him there, putting action to the words he'd spoken about his desire to sit beside her as she took hold of her career meant more than she could say.

It felt as if they'd turned a corner, stepping outside their past and beginning to create the pattern that would tie the rest of their lives together. For the first time the thought of a future with him didn't scare her.

As he walked up beside her, she took his hand.

"You headed over to the setup area too?"

"I am," he said before squeezing her hand in a way that felt reassuring. "If there's anything I can do to help out, let me know."

"I may take you up on that," she replied. "So much to do before I need to get over to Rockliffe at five."

He put his hands out. "I am yours for as long as you need me."

"Speaking of…"

"Hmm?"

"What do you think she's going to ask me?"

He shrugged. "Could be a bunch of different things. Nothing she's said anything to me about. But more importantly, you know you did great in there."

She wasn't sure why Jacob's excitement was important.

Okay, she knew.

He mattered to her. She was safe enough in their relationship to say that she loved him. That she always had. "Thanks," she managed. "I appreciate your support."

"You know you always have it," he replied. "Always." He paused as they headed down the steps of the foundation building, making their way up to the setup area.

"I appreciate that more than I can say.

His smile hit her all the way down to her toes. It filled her with happiness, joy, and love.

"May I kiss you?"

In response, she placed her lips on his, let her hands explore his cheekbones, his hands on her hair, his tongue exploring her mouth. It was perfect, inevitable and she didn't want to let go.

Chapter Twenty-Three

ANNA SMILED AS she stood in the very crowded bedroom she'd spent the summer in.

The last few hours had been wild; how else did she explain a very last-minute invitation to finish the wing exhibit that only happened because the entire town, as well as the people who meant the most to her, had helped?

Thankfully, the docent who had been hired to oversee the exhibit for the duration of the Summer Days festival had been smart and wonderful, which made the opening itself very easy.

And now, Anna, her friends, and her grandmother were all getting dressed for the ball. At her grandmother's house, a far cry from the way they'd all gotten ready at the restaurant for Charlotte's party less than a month ago.

She hugged both Charlotte and Rivvy. "You guys are fantastic. Thank you for sticking by me."

Next she turned to the other important group hug, throwing her arms around both Sarah and Batya. "I'm so very lucky I know both of you. Thank you for being my friends no matter what."

"Or *where*," Batya pointed out. "You know?"

Sarah raised an eyebrow. "Where, huh?"

Anna deliberately ignored the fishing expedition. She wasn't leaving Brooklyn and definitely not moving in with Jacob. She'd be spending more time with him, for sure, but she wasn't going anywhere. Not yet. "I don't know what you're talking about, though if the museum accepts my proposal, I may be doing exhibits onsite with different partners and in the city as well as here on Long Island."

"Oh really?" Charlotte asked. "That's great. So when do we start the registry?"

"There is no registry," Anna said, sighing deeply at her friends. "Not anytime soon. We just got back together again. I'm not even thinking about aisles or ketubahs or dresses. Or rings."

"So…" Oma raised an eyebrow. "You are confirming that there is a relationship. The rest is just noise, especially considering your mother said she and your father left early, but they don't trust the Cross Bronx to be traffic-free, which means they'll be here at some point, and don't want you to worry."

She blinked. "Mom and Dad are coming?"

Oma nodded, and smiled. "Yes, *mamaleh*, your parents are coming."

A great deal about her future was going to be decided that night. And instead of scared, strangely enough, Anna felt she was ready to face it. Whatever it might be.

JACOB HAD BEEN staring out the window, trying to think, trying to focus.

He looked up and saw his mother. Elegant, hair up, a silvery, glittery dress he'd seen her wear many times before and a necklace his father had given her. Pearls, diamond, and hearts. The consummate hostess.

"Yes?" They hadn't spent much time together since he'd gotten back from Texas that wasn't spent on the wing or any of the other random details he had to take care of.

Much to his surprise, his mother smiled. "I'm looking forward to the ball tonight," she said. "Are you?"

He nodded. "So much exciting news, so many things to celebrate."

"I take it you're talking about Anna?"

He shrugged. "New beginnings, new partnerships, new bridges. Yes, she's at the center of it all, but I'm so hopeful about so many other things."

"Even if she doesn't get the offer she wants?"

And here came the conversation he'd expected, the one he'd been putting off. "First of all, don't start with that, because you have something to say about what happens."

"Not as much as you think I do, Jacob."

He shook his head; he wasn't sure what his mother wanted him to believe, but he was definitely not buying it. "Second of all, whatever she wants to do with her career, I'll support her in any way she wants me to. Don't think I won't tie up the archives and use my influence to get her something worthy of her."

His mother raised an eyebrow. "You're already her knight in shining armor riding to battle?"

He blew out a breath. "Not shining, not riding, and not knight. I'm her…fixer. I'm hers. In any capacity she wants me. Even if that means supporting her choice to go to any museum she wants to go to, even one that wouldn't be benefitted by my connections. I mean that."

"I'm sure you do," his mother replied, and much to his surprise there was yet another of his mother's smiles. "I've raised a good man, and that's all I've ever wanted."

"Uh…"

"I know," she replied. "Enough for both of us." And as his mother stepped back, she smiled and checked her phone. "It seems that our guests are here."

"That they are," he said as he took his mother's arm.

THE BALL WAS a dream. It was dotted with yellow, blue, and green balloons, each designed to look like beach balls in order to mirror Isaac's sculpture. Glitter and silver drapes adorned the chairs. The buffet tables were out in full force and people meandered around the room with pretty pastel colored drinks.

"This is beautiful," she said as Jacob came out to meet her.

"I'm glad you like it," he replied.

She looked at him, in his black suit and tie that matched the pink flowers on her dress. He was simply breathtaking, and the way his smile lit up his face made her so very glad she was able to dance with him.

And as the music started, Anna squeezed Jacob's hand. "This is amazing."

"It is. It really is."

"Miss Cohen," interjected the director of the museum with a smile on his face. "I was excited to help yesterday with the opening. You're amazing at organization, and at tons of different programs."

"Thank you," she said softly. She looked around for Jacob, but he'd gone. And yet she knew, deep down, that he'd come back.

"Miss Cohen, I want to inform you that the board of directors went over your proposal and in conjunction with the foundation, I'd like to tell you we approve and would love to welcome you back to the staff at the museum. We'll talk financials and exhibit timelines as well as the details with the head of the foundation sometime next week."

She bit her lip to keep herself from screaming. "Oh wow," she managed. "That's wonderful. Absolutely wonderful. Thank you, sir."

"I'm glad to hear you think so," the director replied, a broad smile on his face. "I look forward to working with you in the future. For now, you should enjoy the party."

And as the museum director went off into the crowd, she made her own way through the party, only to be stopped by her parents. "You're actually here."

"Don't look so surprised," her mother said. "You look gorgeous. Your grandmother is enjoying herself and your father and I are so very proud of you. We saw the exhibit in the wing, and I have to say that I really enjoyed the way you told that story."

She couldn't keep the smile off her face. "I…"

Her parents gave her a huge hug, the corsage clear on her mother's wrist. "We love you," her mother said. "And we support you in whatever choices you make."

JACOB COULDN'T STOP smiling. He'd gone to find Anna the second he'd found out about the job and ended up celebrating alongside Sarah, Isaac, Batya, Tony, Charlotte, Ken, Rivvy, and Anna's family. And he promised he'd have Ken read the contract if she wanted, if she didn't have another attorney in mind.

"It's fine," she said. "It's really fine."

He just couldn't stop staring at her.

"You keep doing that and I'll think something's wrong with me."

He shook his head. "No," he replied. "Not ever. No." He paused. "I'm so lucky. I'm so proud of you and I'm so excited for you."

She raised an eyebrow, and he couldn't help but smile. "Lucky? Proud?"

He nodded back at her, as earnest as he could be. "Both to be in your orbit."

She smiled at him.

He couldn't help it. "You're going to do great things."

"I'm so scared," she said, squeezing his hand. "There's a lot of responsibility in knowing they not only listened to but also accepted my proposal without any reservations or anything."

"But it wasn't without merits," he replied. "You didn't ask for the moon, even though you could have. And honestly, I would have."

"Of course you would have," she said, leaning back into him.

"But you didn't. You asked for something you could reasonably manage. Learning with a boss who understands curation, working with things you enjoy." He shrugged. "No-brainer, especially because you're so good at what you do. And you're a good person any museum would want…any person would want to associate with."

There was a beat of silence as his heart pounded, waiting for her to reply. "You really think so?"

"I do," he said. "I absolutely do." Then he took her hand, led her back to her friends, and the beginning of this new chapter of their lives.

Chapter Twenty-Four

One year later

JACOB MADE A last adjustment on his tie, reached for the jacket that sat on the hanger, and thought of Anna. She was getting ready at her grandmother's house, catching up with friends and family, leaving him here at Rockliffe.

In the same place where he'd gotten ready for the Summer Days Ball a year before.

Anna had settled into her job, they'd traveled together, she'd even done an exhibit for the Grove of the dreidels they'd commissioned, just as she'd predicted a year before. So many different exhibits, each partnered with the museum and others across the country.

It wasn't easy, juggling their schedules, but it was worth it. It was perfect for them.

And tonight as he put on his jacket, he reached for the box that sat on the dresser. The one that had their whole future wrapped in a box. The real reason he'd insisted on getting ready here at Rockliffe. Carefully, easily, he put the box in his inside pocket.

"So it's tonight? You're going to ask?"

He raised an eyebrow as his mother came to join him in the sitting room.

"Oh come on, Jacob," his mother replied, resplendent in gold. "I'm thrilled you're happy. Who was it that arranged for those playdates all those years ago? Who…"

"You also separated us unnecessarily."

His mother didn't deny it. "You had to be better, you had to be socially aware in a way your father wasn't. You needed to be aware enough to deserve her, and you needed to be aware enough to understand why that was so important."

Those were words he had to think over, not then, but later. "Thank you? I guess?"

His mother smiled again, the kind of smile that accompanied one of her laughs. "Aaah yes. You *guess*, huh?"

"More than guess."

His mother put her arms around him, briefly, careful not to lean against the ring. And after a while, after they'd caught up with everybody, he asked Anna if she wanted to get some air. "You know," he said, "go out on the balcony."

She smiled. "Anywhere with you," she said.

Obliging her, and his own heavily beating heart, he took her hand and led her out onto the balcony.

He nodded. "Actually…" He swallowed and got himself ready. "There's something I wanted to talk to you about."

She turned around and he stepped away, holding the box behind his back. "What…is there a problem?"

"No." He paused, and took a deep breath. "Something else. A question that takes into account our history, our lives and our loves. And reminds us both that we have a future, or at least I'd like us to."

She covered her eyes, and she started to wipe them. Tears and mascara came away in her fingertips. "Are you...?"

"I don't know what you think," he said, as he reached out a finger to brush some of the tears away, "but there's a question I'd like to ask you, if you'd let me. It's...a big one. And...it brings requirements, obligations, and a whole bunch of things."

"Does it come with you?

He blinked. "What?"

"Does the question, the one you're clearly afraid to ask, come with you?"

"I..."

"Go ahead and ask it then, my love" she replied, smiling. "Because you'll never know what my answer will be unless and until you ask it."

His heart was pounding. He'd never been so nervous in his life. So he held his breath and in the beginning of June, on the balcony at Rockliffe, got down on one knee. "Will you, Anna Cohen, make me the happiest man in the world? Will you marry me?"

Her face lit up like a menorah, like a marshmallow at a campfire. Like diamonds. "Yes."

He couldn't answer; he couldn't even fumble the box to

open it. "I…"

This time it was her, leaning toward him, and he felt her fingers brush against his face. "I get to be yours for the rest of our lives. That's all I wanted, you know? I love you, Jacob, and once we figured ourselves out, all I wanted was to be yours. I'd marry you with a ring the same material we used to make swords when we were kids, you know?"

He laughed. Of course she'd make him remember the childhood that bound them together right now. "Paper, huh?"

She nodded, her eyes sparkling. "Paper. Yes."

Now he opened the box. Now he was ready to show her and he hoped his hand wasn't going to shake. "This ring isn't paper," he said, making sure she saw the thin gold band with the small diamond surrounded by royal blue sapphires. "But," he continued, "it's history in a way that you'd appreciate. It belonged to my great-great-grandmother, the one who helped to build the synagogue, the one who recognized the importance of our culture and our history."

She cried as he slipped it on. "I…"

He pulled her close to him, and even in the early fire of summer, he sat down, her on his lap, letting her cry on his shoulder. "We'll choose a ring that you feel comfortable wearing after tonight, but tonight, here, for this ball, I wanted you to wear this one. Because I couldn't help myself, I couldn't stop thinking about it."

He heard her sniff, breaking the silence after he'd spoken, and when she looked up at him he carefully wiped a tear away from her face. "You knew I'd appreciate it."

He nodded.

And she helped him stand, put her arms around him.

And when she kissed him, the familiarity of her, the feel of her mouth, and her unique taste reminded him how much she'd always been home for him. No matter what the world around them looked like.

And when he pulled back, the brightness in his eyes made her smile. "Let's go inside."

He nodded. "Wouldn't miss it."

And with her hand in his, the next chapter in their history had begun. And he couldn't wait to see what their happy ending would look like.

The End

Want more? Check out Sarah and Isaac's story in *Miracles and Menorahs*!

Join Tule Publishing's newsletter for more great reads and weekly deals!

Author's Note

History is important, and the lens through which it's seen even more so. Ms. Beverly Jenkins, a brilliant bestselling author of historical romance, said at a daylong conference held at the Library of Congress in 2015, and multiple times afterwards, when talking about why it's important for her to write African-American historical romance set in the United States despite the difficult history of African-Americans in this country 'we are our ancestors' happy endings.'

This quote stayed with me years later, and the idea forms the core of the way I approached this story.

Now to separate fact from fiction:
Neither the Truitts nor this version of the Horowitz-Margaretens are real.

But the history these Horowitz-Margaretens detail in the course of the story is true. The story of Rockliffe was heavily inspired by the story of Oheka Castle, built between 1914 and 1919 in West Hills New York, a hamlet of Huntington. Otto Kahn didn't separate the land Oheka was built on from the rest of Huntington, or tear a room off the house to create a Jewish Center, but the story of Oheka itself is the story that inspired the building of Rockliffe. And a lot of this story.

The design for Rockliffe wasn't inspired by Oheka Castle, but by the much smaller and much more 'manageable' Old Westbury Gardens, located in Old Westbury, New York.

The town of Rockliffe Manor is an interesting hodge-podge of Briarcliff Manor and Huntington, New York. The Briarcliff part was increased in importance considering how long it's been since I've been able to visit Long Island.

The specific flavor of anti-Semitism Jacob and his family deal with and have dealt with all through the years is also real. All you have to do to see it, is think about the fact that George Soros was the only person who wasn't a politician who received a mail bomb in October of 2018. Each time people jokingly refer to getting their 'Soros money' they are giving credence to an anti-Semitic conspiracy theory. See also recent discussions about people who believe influential Jews own space lasers. Each of these are spun from the same thread of a conspiracy theory and no matter how funny they may sound, they are serious.

JIDS is also not real. It is heavily inspired by organizations like the Young Center, RAICES Texas and HIAS. They each do amazing work.

So does Rabbi Sandra Lawson. Rabbi Lawson is one of the many clergy members who inspired me during this period of time, and thusly inspired Rabbi Davidson.

The museums listed in the book aren't real, but the

Manhattan Museum of Jewish History is heavily inspired by the Center for Jewish History, located on West 16th Street in New York. It houses five different cultural archives and loads of different exhibitions.

Acknowledgments

The first thing I need to say here is that I stand on the shoulders of giants. Zoe Archer, Alina Adams, Rose Lerner, as well as specifically for this book, Kelley Armstrong, Lynn Kurland, Beverly Jenkins, and Evelyn Vaughn. Without them, and the stories they wrote and continue to write, this book wouldn't exist.

This book was entirely written during the period from May to August of 2020, and revised from September 2020 to January 2021. Which means that most of what I saw as I was writing this was the interior of my bedroom.

That I got actual locations on Long Island written with any degree of accuracy when all I could see was said bedroom wall in Westchester is because of the many drives and moments I've spent with Kimberly Rocha, Vivi Parish, Jennifer Gracen, Jeannie Moon, Meara Platt, L.A. Bryce, Blue Saffire, Patty Blount, Nika Rhone, Miranda Wolfe, Christine Woinich, the members of the Book Obsessed Chicks book club, and so many others. I had other plans for the writing of this book, but when it's safe again I need a Briermere pie and in person time with all of you. :D

And speaking of Vivi, your inspirational photos and a trip to Philly shaped Jacob in a way I never could have imagined. Thank you <3

And Kim, most of these drives were spent with you. I wouldn't know the beauty of Westbury Gardens or the joys of Greenport and stopping to see sunflowers without you, my friend. Anna and Jacob's summer drives and adventures have roots in ours. I cannot wait for more.

I also need time with my Westchester writers—Falguni Kothari, Kwana Jackson, and Laura K. Curtis—next time we get together is in a yarn store!

Speaking of yarn stores, my Sunday zoom knitting crew did more than they knew to keep me sane during this period. Thank you <3 Those two hours are so important.

Lydia San Andres and Steve Ammidown both talked to me about archives and museum work. Any mistakes are mine.

Ceillie Simkiss answered the call when I needed help accessing a document that wasn't in a format I could access. When life is better and it's safer, you and I will have some pie. ☺

Amy Jo Cousins made time in her busy schedule to talk to me about the day-to-day operations and the work of the Young Center. I asked her about a bunch of different things, including what kind of financial contributions would make the organization's life easier, and what those kind of hands-on contributions would go to. Her answers informed the work Jacob did with the Mitzvah Alliance, and any mistakes made are mine.

The actual writing was done mostly with Zoom sprints. My New York Romance Rogues, especially Alexis Daria, Lucy Eden, Rebecca Heffner, Adriana Herrera, Robin Lovett, Tori Luce, Celestine Martin, Harper Miller, and Eden Royce were a great support system. As were the members of the 30Day Drafters group, led by Lyssa Kay Adams. Our weekly sprints were invaluable, and I treasure those moments. Laura Hunsaker, Sara Rider, Alys Murray, Morgan Routh and Cassandra Carr also held my hand during this drafting process.

Julie Sturgeon is a brilliant editor, and she nailed exactly what this book needed to be. Thank you :D

Fortune Whelan, Nan Reinhardt, Jadesola James, and Melanie Ting were wonderful sprint partners through the revision process, and some of the amazing members of the Romance Schmooze group were also wonderful sprint partners when I was under the revision timeline.

Chatting with the members of the Romance Schmooze group is always, by the way, always reinvigorating <3 Kol Ha Kavod to all of us, always <3

Michelle Lawson read this book multiple times in various formats, and when I say that I do not think I could have managed to get through this book without Felicia Grossman's handholding, I mean every single word.

And speaking of Felicia, she and Elizabeth Kahn were

amazing to tolerate me during the organization process of the Love All Year anthology. Elizabeth, I tell you nothing would have happened without you and I am so very lucky I know you.

The same for extremely distracted me during the June release of 'Roughing It'; Laura Hunsaker, Heather Lire, and Isabo Kelly were and always are rock stars. I can't wait to do it again :D

Knowing that Lynnette Novak is in my corner makes everything easier. Thank you for being my agent and for believing in me even when I don't believe in myself.

To everybody at Tule: Nikki Babri for all the work you do, Cyndi Parent for answering all of my ridiculous questions, and Jane Porter—the guiding light and guiding force, your belief in me and my words is humbling. I am so very proud to be a Tule author.

And to everybody who stocked, read, loved, talked about, wrote about, created beautiful posts about, recommended, added to subscription boxes, hosted events for, joined events for, suggested and hosted book clubs about *Miracles and Men*orahs, know that all of this sustained me when things were difficult. You put so much love into the book, and I felt every single bit of it. I'm a former bookseller and reviewer, and I know from personal experience that what you do is hard. ***I do not take your support for granted***. There are so many books that get released each day, and there is very little time in the day to spend on new titles, the fact you spent any time on mine means so much. Thank you. <3

And to anybody who's taken this journey with me, thank you <3 I adore you.

To Marnie McMahon and Megan Walski—I can write good friends because I have them. Thank you for being mine. I am so very lucky both of you are in my life. ☺ I cannot wait to see you in person again.

To Russ (who barely missed being asked all the questions). You are inspiring and I am so very happy you are my brother. You and Marisa bring so much joy to my life and the time I get to spend with Elijah is a blessing. ☺

To my parents, who taught me history and taught me to be proud of who I am and where I come from. Thank you. I love you.

If you enjoyed *History of Us*,
you'll love the next book in the....

Friendships and Festivals series

Book 1: *Miracles and Menorahs*

Book 2: *History of Us*

Book 3: *Love and Latkes*
Coming October 2021!

Available now at your favorite online retailer!

About the Author

Stacey Agdern is an award-winning former bookseller who has reviewed romance novels in multiple formats and given talks about various aspects of the romance genre. She incorporates Jewish characters and traditions into her stories so that people who grew up like she did can see themselves take center stage on the page. She's also a member of both LIRW and RWA NYC. She lives in New York, not far from her favorite hockey team's practice facility.

Thank you for reading

History of Us

If you enjoyed this book, you can find more from all our great authors at TulePublishing.com, or from your favorite online retailer.

TULE
PUBLISHING

CPSIA information can be obtained
at www.ICGtesting.com
Printed in the USA
LVHW092149040621
689285LV00021B/223

9 781953 647955